The Stolen

Passport

JIMMY DUNNE

Copyrights ©2025 by Jimmy Dunne

All Rights Reserved.

No part of this book may be reproduced or transmitted in any form by any means, electronic or mechanical, including photocopying and recording, or by any information storage and retrieval system, except as may be expressly permitted in writing from the author.

Dedication

As always.

This book is dedicated to my wife, Marian

(The love of my life)

Dedication

To my Grandchildren.

Noah Byrne

Zack Byrne

Chloe Byrne

Olivia Dunne

Isabella Dunne

Love you always... Jimmy

Acknowledgements

I feel it takes a village to raise a child. I also think it takes a whole community to aid a person in writing a book because of the encouragement and support I received from my friends, family, and comrades.

To my son Damien for his invaluable help, which was given to me gladly in his assistance with technical support (my nemesis), cover design, and contents of this book.

I am grateful to our writing facilitator, Aoife Kerrigan, who constantly challenged me to make this story the best it could be.

To my fellow members of the IUNVA Creative Writing Group, for your support.

My niece, Leah Hensey, for being an insightful and supportive proofreader of my book.

My daughter Jenny, for your love and encouragement in early drafts of this book.

My Son Martin, who enthusiastically got behind my writing endeavours.

My sister, Noeleen, who supplied me with material for the cover design.

My sister Margaret, for your unwavering support.

Irish United Nations Association, I.U.N.V.A., for your assistance and support.

Organisation of National Ex-Service Personnel, O.N.E., for your comradeship.

And of course, my wife Marian, for your infinite patience, help, and advice, in bringing my third book to print.

And a very big thank you to anyone who picks up my book. I hope you enjoy it, and I'd really appreciate it if you would tell others and help spread the word if you did. It would also be great if you would post a review.

Many thanks. Jimmy

Table of Contents

THE STOLEN PASSPORT

By Jimmy Dunne

1

Gasping for air.

Footsteps running.

Running ...

Running.

Heart pounding in her chest, echoing in her ears. A mist before her eyes block her vision; she is disoriented as she runs. In her outstretched hand, she can see her passport bobbing up and down as her pace quickens.

She calls out, "Please wait ... please ... hold the gate."

Her pleas echo in her ears. As she runs, the mist begins to clear ahead. Yes, someone is holding the door, encouraging her to hurry; she is almost there. As she races through the open door, she recognises the lady holding it. She cannot believe her eyes; it's her grandmother smiling at her as she passes. Then Mary's eyes open from the dream, her heavy breathing abates as the steward announces over the Tannoy:

"Ladies and gentlemen, welcome to Dublin. The local time now is six am. Please remain in your seats with your seat belt securely fastened until the aircraft has come to a complete standstill."

While the steward continued with his spiel, it all turned to gibberish as her stomach churned. Mary quickly grabbed the plastic bag she was holding throughout the flight and vomited. It wasn't the first time this had happened during her eight-hour flight from Chicago. She had used the toilet three or four times during the night. Morning sickness had hit her hard, and she was glad to be getting off the plane soon to get some fresh Irish air into her lungs. As Mary walked through passport control, she had to be careful to show her own passport while keeping the other one hidden in her pants. She should have dumped the other passport but decided to keep it; at this moment, she couldn't think why. Then she saw a sign on the wall that read, "Welcome to Ireland," and Mary smiled to herself and thought,

"I've made it home, I'm free of him at last, and most of all, I'm safe, and so is my baby."

2

She had no luggage with her and nothing to collect from the carousel; the only clothes she had were what she stood up in. She had changed what was left of her dollars in O'Hare airport to euros, which didn't amount to much. She wondered if it would be enough to get a taxi home to Castleknock if she decided to go there. It had been four years since she had left home to go to America on a J1 visa, and the price of a taxi must have changed since then. She also knew she couldn't return to the USA as she had overstayed her visa. But she had no intention of going back anyway. She stopped for a second and asked herself the same question again...

"Should I go home, or should I keep running?"

The question echoed in her head repeatedly as she walked out into the terminal in a trance. The aroma of freshly brewed coffee coming from a restaurant smelled delicious, so Mary decided to sit down and ponder her next move. She knew nobody would know of her whereabouts at this very moment, so she could take as much time as she needed. As Mary relaxed with her coffee and freshly baked croissant, she noticed people stealing a glance at her but would look away quickly when caught. Then she looked at her reflection in the mirror opposite her. As a habit, she had formed to make sure she wasn't being followed, she checked that there was nobody behind her. She took a good look at herself and her appearance. Mary was horrified and couldn't believe the sight before her. She had tired, sunken eyes and looked totally dishevelled. Then, despairingly, she asked herself the question. Was this the same eighteen-year-old girl so full of life who left this airport four years earlier for a one-year adventure to America? As she studied herself now at the age of twenty-two, she could see a sophisticated, attractive, slim girl. She was about five feet four with long blonde hair tied in a ponytail and sporting a baseball cap. Her tracksuit was looking tired from travelling constantly for the last thirty-six hours when her plan came together to go on the run. She knew what she needed now was a hot soak in a bathtub and a few hours' sleep. Then, putting on some makeup and a change of clothes, she would look a whole lot better. But for now, all she wanted to do was savour her hot coffee as she pondered how it all went so horribly wrong and how lucky she was to be sitting here now, leaving her terrible ordeal behind.

3

As Mary cast her mind back, she remembered the morning sun, which was shining through the plane's windows and the excitement as she made her way down the aisle to find her seat on the big Boeing 737. Mary had flown many times before, usually with her parents or auntie on short-haul flights. But this was different; this time she was flying on her first adventure alone, and it was transatlantic. When she got to her seat, she struggled to put her case into the overhead. As she tried to push it up, suddenly, a big pair of hands came from behind her to assist in securing her bag. Mary turned to thank the person who helped her; she was greeted with a big smile from a very handsome man not much older than herself. He would be sitting beside her for the flight to LAX and introduced himself as Brian, so Mary did the same. For the next 12 hours, they slept, ate, and got to know each other. In his soft Donegal accent, Brian told Mary that he had received a scholarship from the West Coast

University and was studying and playing football for the American Career College in Irvine. He explained that there was a big Irish community (*diaspora*) on the West Coast. He continued that he had finished his first year in business studies and was returning to Los Angeles after being home to take care of a bit of business in his hometown. Mary explained that she was going to America to stay with her friend for a year and have an adventure. Hopefully, she would get a job as a barmaid quickly to earn enough money to go touring around and see as many sights as possible. She told Brian she had a lot of experience as a barmaid and barista in her family's bar and restaurant business in Tenerife. She continued, she lived and studied in Ireland and spent all her summer and winter holidays in Tenerife working behind the bar. Mary told him as her eyes glistened with excitement. Now that she has finished her exams, it was time to stretch her wings and see what the world had to offer.

Then she added, "I can also mix a mean cocktail."

When they landed in LAX, Brian and Mary parted company, promising to keep in touch. They exchanged phone numbers and home addresses, which were not very far apart from where they were staying. They hugged each other before saying goodbye, waving, and exchanging last glances. Mary's friend June was waiting and saw them parting. She enquired enviously about the gorgeous guy Mary had been hugging. Mary, pleased with herself, replied that they had met on the plane and were going to keep in touch. June replied,

"I hope he has a twin brother," as they both laughed and headed for the car park.

In the car, June and Mary babbled away as June explained about where they were going to live and about the neighbourhood and bars in the vicinity. She spoke about the gorgeous beaches nearby and all the fabulous hunky guys strutting their stuff. When June turned on the playlist very loudly on the radio, they both sang together, screaming and bopping in their seats. As they bopped along, Mary thought about how this was going to be the most exciting year ever. Then Brian's smiling face flashed in her mind again.

4

When they got to their apartment, Mary was surprised at how small it was. In fact, it was so small, she wondered where she was going to sleep. June laughed when she saw the reaction on her face. She told her not to worry as she showed her the hideaway guest bed that pulled out from beneath hers, which turned it into a double. There was a small kitchen in the corner with a two-ring hob, a kettle, and a microwave. There was a tiny shower-room and toilet that had only room for one person. The two girls laughed together as they bounced on the beds, holding each other's hands. They knew that their adventure was only beginning, and as June said,

"It was small, but it is cheap."

June, like Mary, had an athletic body with long auburn hair and beautiful brown eyes. She had high cheekbones, which accentuated her button nose and luscious lips. She was a friendly, outgoing girl and was always ready to greet you with a smile. She worked as a second-hand car salesperson, which suited her personality perfectly. She had learned her trade through her father's motor business back in Ireland. Her father, who was well-known and respected in the industry, had gotten her the big job through his contacts. Mary knew she would have to find work immediately, as the two schoolmates intended to save as much as possible to go on a road trip together before the year's end. The next morning after June left for work, Mary rang her mother, Rose. She explained about her flat and how small it was but couldn't wait to get out and about to find a job. After hanging up, she decided to pack her things away, tidy her bed, and then explore her surroundings. She was just about finished when her phone rang, and she was surprised and delighted to hear Brian's voice. He said that he had the day off, and as it was her first day in the USA, he offered to show her around. Mary was happy but wasn't sure where to meet him as she didn't know her neighbourhood yet. Brian said there was no problem as he would pick her up from her flat within the hour. As Mary hung up, she smiled to herself and swung around in delight. An hour later, as Mary waited outside her apartment, Brian pulled up in a big red flashy convertible Mustang that matched the colour of his red hair. When he pulled into the curb, he called out to her with his beautiful smile, saying,

"Your chariot awaits my lady."

Mary couldn't believe her luck as they drove away with the wind in her hair, sitting beside such a handsome man.

5

Brian was the perfect gentleman; he showed her all the sights of LA. Whenever they stopped, he would jump out and hold the door for her. He drove along the coast, and then they stopped for a lovely lunch in a fancy restaurant. When he spoke to her, he kept complete eye contact. It made her feel like she was the only person in the restaurant. In the afternoon, he brought her back to his college and showed her around the campus. He showed her the sports area where he played football and introduced her to some of his teammates. Mary marvelled at their height and physique as she thought to herself, June would be mad jealous when I tell her where I was and the company I was keeping. Later, as they walked around, Brian suggested they go into the clubhouse as he wanted Mary to meet his coach. Mary couldn't believe the size of the place and how plush it was. To her, it felt like a four-star hotel with carpeted floors, rows and rows of glass display cabinets with all sorts of medals, photos, and silverware. When they went into the lounge area, Brian's coach was sitting in a booth. He had all kinds of game connotation sheets spread out on the table before him and was studying them hard as they approached.

Brian cleared his throat respectfully to let him know they were there. The coach lifted his head, and Mary studied him before he spoke. She saw a man in his late 60s, his silver hair framing his face, which told the story of resilience and weathered, wrinkled strength. His hands, though aged and spotted, were strong and steady which tended to young men's injuries and battle scars on the field of play. His demeanour was a blend of strength and gentleness as he spoke. Mary could feel his soft but firm voice reflecting the wisdom he had gained through his coaching years. Brian introduced Mary, saying to his coach that she was the girl he had spoken to him about. His broad, gentle smile lit up his face as he took Mary's hand in his and told her to call him Ed.

"Well, young lady, you are the girl that can make a mean cocktail, so I've been reliably informed by this young man here," while glancing at Brian.

Mary, feeling the softness and warmth of his hand in hers, relaxed immediately. She smiled back at Ed and said she had plenty of experience since she was a child working in her parents' bars.

"Is that so, Ed replied, well you go behind that there bar and mix me a Tom Collins while I talk field tactics to Brian."

Mary liked the challenge, so she immediately went behind the bar as instructed. When she returned with his drink, Ed slowly tasted the liquor, savouring it in his mouth momentarily. When he swallowed, he smiled at Mary, saying,

"Madam, this is one of the best Tom Collins I have tasted in years".

Then he asked.

"When can you start?"

Mary looked up at Brian quizzically. Brian just held out his arms in defeat and smiled, so Mary suggested,

"Would tomorrow night be, ok?

Ed replied with a smile on his wrinkled face,

"The sooner the better. But don't go making too many cocktails for this young feller, as I need him in tip-top shape for this weekend," and they all laughed together.

Mary turned and hugged Brian there and then, as she did so, Ed hollered,

"What about me? As I gave you the job, don't I get a hug also?"

Mary flung her arms around Ed, hugging him as he exclaimed laughingly,

"God, I wish I were forty years younger."

Mary had got her first job in America.

6

As Brian showed Mary around the campus, he explained. As an employee, she could use all the facilities available, including the gym and dining hall, plus the Olympic-sized swimming pool. Mary was thrilled about this as she loved swimming most of all, and it also had a huge library. He walked her around the manicured track & field area, and afterwards, he showed her the living quarters where he stayed. Mary was amazed at the size of the whole campus, saying it would take her a few weeks to find out where everything was. She turned to thank Brian for all he did for her. As their eyes met, they kissed ever so softly, and Mary's heart melted. That evening, Brian dropped her off at her apartment block. Mary asked if he would like to come up for coffee. Brian, being the perfect gentleman, gratefully thanked her but said he had to get back to his studies and training. He told her, now that she was working near him, he could see her anytime when she came to work, as they kissed again. Brian drove away as

Mary stood by the curb waving until he was out of sight. Afterwards, she waltzed up the stairs to her flat. June was already home when she let herself in, and Mary regaled her about the whole day's events, including the kiss. June was delighted for her friend and the fact that she had gotten a great job with so many perks. Also, the fact that she was going to be around so many hunky guys, and maybe she would introduce her to a few. They both giggled and laughed together as they spoke about their plans well into the night while lying in bed.

Mary's first days were very busy trying to find her way around and getting used to the setup and her work colleagues. The bar mainly sold high-energy drinks and fruit, as well as milkshakes, coffee, and soft drinks. The lounge was for faculty staff, campus employees, and senior students, with strict rules on alcohol being served to anyone underage. Mary settled in quickly and loved working in the lounge. She was the first proper mixologist they ever had in the college. She quickly became very popular mixing cocktails and mocktails from a list she had prepared and displayed on the bar. Ed was one of her favourite customers and treated her like one of his grandchildren.

Mary noticed that Brian hadn't visited the lounge since she started work and had missed him. She inquired from Ed as to why he never came by. Ed replied that once Brian achieves his grades and turns up for training, he doesn't really keep a check on the team. He continued with a frown, but most of the boys, like all young men, feel they have to party hard every chance they get. He continued while shaking his head, they think they have something to prove. Mary accepted Ed's answer but was still disappointed Brian hadn't come in to see her. It was the following weekend before Brian appeared, and the bar was bustling. Mary had no time to stop and chat with customers. It was about eight pm when a big group of noisy students entered the lounge. Brian was one of them, and Mary's heart skipped a beat when she saw him. There were eight people at the party, four guys and four girls. She noticed that Brian seemed to be the most popular person in the group. The girls were swanning all over him, and Mary felt a twinge of jealousy. As she looked up from time to time over at Brian, their eyes met. He smiled and waved over at Mary but then carried on talking and laughing with the group, so Mary continued serving her customers. Ed, who was sitting at the bar as usual, noticed Mary's reaction to Brian. He advised her not to get too attached to Brian as he had a different agenda and road to journey than she had. He told her to stick to her plan of working, travelling, and experiencing life's memories while she was here. Mary knew Ed was being kind, offering his advice, but was still disappointed as she smiled at Ed, slipping him his favourite cocktail on the house. When Mary had finished her shift, she waited by the curb for June to pick her up as she often did. Suddenly, out of nowhere, Brien appeared like a ghost and gave her an awful fright. Brian just laughed at Mary's reaction to him appearing like that. As Mary recovered her composure, Brian asked her how she was getting on in her new job.

Mary, more composed and happier to see Brian, told him she was settling in fine and thanked him again for getting her the job. But as she spoke, she noticed that Brian's demeanour was different from when she had met him previously. His eyes were wider, and his pupils brighter than usual. While they talked, he seemed to be staring intently at her with a silly grin on his face while moving into Mary's space, which made her feel uncomfortable.

Just then, June's car pulled up beside them, and Mary was glad as Brian backed off. All the way home, Mary was lost in her thoughts about her encounter with Brian. She felt that something was not right with their meeting, and it was a little scary the way he had appeared out of nowhere like that. But she was still delighted to see him again.

7

Unlike her mother, Rose, Mary never really felt that she was psychic. Her mother would talk to her about her having visions as a child, how she would tell Rose of being able to see her late grandparents, Neil and Mary, also about her late uncle Bill, who married her grandfather Neil after her grandmother's death. Mary would cast her mind back to those times; she would remember seeing them in the distance as she played her imaginary little games with her dolls. Or, when she was out and about on her trike, as she rode down the promenade in Tenerife, where she spent her school holidays. They would all be sitting together drinking coffee and would wave happily as she passed by. That was long ago now, and those visions had long since left her as she grew up. But from time to time, when things got stressful, like taking her exams, etc., Mary felt that her grandmother, also called Mary, would visit her in her sleep. She would give her encouraging looks to keep on trying harder. And indeed, it was on that very night that Mary dreamt her grandmother did visit her in her sleep with a worried look on her face. The next morning, Mary woke and felt that something was wrong, but not being able to comprehend what it was, she shook it off. She had a hot shower and got herself ready to explore the city. June had already left for work, and as she sat alone eating breakfast, her phone rang. She saw her mother's name on the screen and was filled with dread as the vision of her grandmother's face came back into her mind. She answered immediately, asking.

"Is everything alright, mum?"

Her mother answered in her usual high-pitched, happy tone,

"Hi pet, of course it is, I just had a fucking terrible night's sleep. So, while I was sitting here having a cup of coffee, I decided to phone my favourite daughter for a chat."

Then Rose asked affectionately,

"Well, how the fuck are ya?"

Her mother loved using profanities. Relieved, Mary smiled at her mother's usual filthy, but friendly way of talking. She immediately went into all the details of her new job, meeting Brian, and her new friend and mentor, Ed. As she spoke, she felt the first pangs of homesickness and was delighted her mother had called. As the call ended, though, she had gotten the feeling that Rose did not really ring her for a chat. Mary thought she had asked a lot of questions about her surroundings and who she was seeing at that moment. It was more like she was pumping her for information, instead of chatting. Her mother, Rose, was a very extroverted lady; she was in her 40s and kept herself in good shape. She always wore the latest fashion, designer clothes, manicured nails, professional makeup, a gold Rolex watch, and Jimmy Choo stilettos. She was part-owner with her father Frank, her aunt Sheila, and uncle Joe of two successful drag bars/restaurants in Tenerife, off the West Coast of Africa. She was also front of house person and a compare. She did indeed speak with a filthy tongue that might put a person off when they met her first, but a more loving and caring person you could not meet.

Frank, her husband, and the same age as Rose, was the financial controller of the business, but his main occupation was based in Dublin. He was an executive in the Irish Financial Services Centre. They were a very loving, dynamic couple who were always seen together holding hands at all the important governmental and presidential functions. They traversed between the Canary Islands and their home in Castleknock, Dublin, where Mary received her education. Mary also worked in the bar during her school holidays, learning her trade and how the business was run.

8

The Queen Vick 1 & 2 was a great place to grow up. Mary longed for her school holidays each year and each semester. She yearned for the excitement, lights, noise, and flamboyant drag Queens wearing stage makeup. The general madness of the place and the fun of working behind the bar with her aunt Sheila were electric. Sheila had taught her everything about mixing cocktails and flicking bottles while customers whooped and clapped at her performance. She also loved sitting around and chatting late into the night with everyone after closing time. When it got too late, her uncle Joe, their stage manager, would insist she go to bed before throwing her over his shoulder to take her laughingly back to their villa. The five partners were Sheila, Conchita, Joe, Frank, and Rose. Joe wasn't really her uncle, but he was still a friend and partner of Queen Vick.

Joe grew up next door to her mother and auntie Sheila back in Stoneybatter, Dublin, before deciding to emigrate to Tenerife to help start up the business. He was in his early 50s, with a receding hairline and a comb over; he was more conventional in the way he dressed. A confirmed bachelor, Joe never really went out with girls. Mary remembered, he always loved her aunt Sheila. He once proposed to Sheila, but Sheila had already fallen in love with her long-time partner, Conchita. She was already living in Tenerife, where they had their own apartment.

Conchita Martinez was the bank manager for the Banco Vistasur Canarias. She, with Frank, looked after the day-to-day finances of the company. Mary would stay with them from time to time, and they would spoil her with days out and shopping for clothes, etcetera. If there was a Canarian festival on, and there were many, they always brought Mary and would make a big fuss of her. Conchita was an exquisite Canarian lady who taught Mary how to read, write, and speak Spanish, which Mary majored in during her college exams. When Conchita was working in the bank, she always wore her beautiful, long black hair tied up in a bun. She was tall and slim and would wear a body-hugging formal business suit with crisp white blouse above a pencil skirt, and stilettos to accentuate her lovely long legs.

But when Conchita was off duty, she dressed much more casually. Her beautiful, black, shiny hair would hang loosely over her shoulders, held back by designer sunglasses perched on her head. She would wear a loose t-shirt with tight blue jeans above elegant, beaded sandals.

Auntie Sheila, Rose's sister, was a little more butch in her appearance. She had worked in fancy hotels and bars as a silver service waitress since she left school. She was slightly more timid and gentler. She liked to dress in darker colour clothes, maroon bovver boots, ankle-length black jeans, and a black aviator jacket. She liked piercings and had a few tattoos on show above her studded black leather watch strap. Her short black hair was always cut and cropped to shoulder length, depending on the Tenerife climate and humidity.

Put together, they were a very unconventional family, but they were all caring and loving to each other. Mary loved every one of them dearly for the way they had nurtured, protected, and educated her during her happy childhood. They were the five owners and business partners of the thriving Queen Vick 1 & 2, which was started nearly 14 years previously by her grandfather, Neil and his husband Bill, who were ex-military chefs in both the Irish and British armies. They met while on peacekeeping duty in Cyprus years previously and married after they both retired. Neil had been happily married to her grandmother, Mary, Rose and Sheila's mother, until her passing. Then, after that, and needing companionship, they formed their own partnership and fell in love as their friendship grew. As their business became more successful, they formed their own family partnership so they could expand. And to this day, the Queen Vick 1 & 2 has gone from strength to strength. They both passed away within weeks of each other when Mary was about four years old. That is why Rose would remind her about her vision of seeing them both with her grandmother along the promenade when she was younger. And Rose knew, like her, she had psychic powers. But now sitting here at her table in Dublin airport, looking into her empty coffee cup, wringing her hands, Mary asked herself again and again,

"What am I to do?"

"What is my next move?"

"Where will I go?"

"Do I keep running?"

"Maybe I could board another plane to England and have an abortion?"

"Yes." Maybe that is the answer. Nobody knows my condition or my whereabouts. If I had an abortion, I could get on with my life, start afresh, so to speak. Lost in her thoughts, Mary pondered the question repeatedly.

Suddenly, she was snapped out of her conundrum as her mother appeared standing beside her and bellowed,

"Mary, what the fuck are you doing here?"

Mary, totally shocked in disbelief, looked up from her coffee cup to see her mother standing in front of her, holding the same look of disbelief as she did. Everything around them froze as they looked into each other's eyes for what seemed like minutes. Then Mary broke down as an enormous sob came up from her throat, crying out,

"Mom, ooh mom," as she broke down into tears.

Rose didn't say a word; she just wrapped her arms lovingly around her only daughter, and she hugged her as she uncontrollably sobbed and sobbed into the side of her neck. People looked on and spoke in hushed tones as Rose consoled Mary. She hugged her even more tightly because her heart was breaking for her child at this very moment to see her so distraught. After about 15 minutes, when Mary calmed down, she lifted her head to look at her mother, Rose, again, in total disbelief that she was there. Rose just smiled back at Mary, saying,

"Come on, let's go home."

Mary, drying her eyes, and without saying a word, nodded in agreement as they left arm in arm. Not one word was spoken on the journey home to Castleknock. Rose was just grateful that her daughter was sitting beside her, for she knew she could leave the explanations until later. Mary, lost in her thoughts, was wondering how the hell she ended up in her mother's car? Or even more strangely, how the hell did she know she was in Dublin airport at that very moment, sitting at that very table? As they stood in the hallway of their home, Rose looked at Mary's dishevelled state and suggested a bath! Mary nodded in agreement, and they both went upstairs. When the water was ready, Rose peeped around Mary's bedroom door to let her know. She saw her daughter fully clothed, thrown across her bed, fast asleep. Rose just covered her up and tiptoed out of the room, thinking to herself,

"She's home, safe now, so nothing else matters."

Then she stopped momentarily on the landing, while looking up to the heavens, she said,

"Thanks, ma'am, I know it was you."

9

When Rose returned downstairs, she was very agitated and couldn't settle. She paced around the kitchen, trying to find something to do or clean. She knew it was too late now for her spinning session in the gym. So, as she was already in her tracksuit and runners, she decided to go for a jog in the Phoenix Park to clear her head. She was trying to make sense of it all and asked herself the same question repeatedly.

"What the fuck happened this morning?"

As Rose entered the Phoenix Park gates, the whole vista opened before her. Green trees, open space, fresh air, where she could breathe, stretch her legs, and clear her mind. As she jogged alone in the quietness of the park, she looked down from time to time at her white runners. Hearing the thump thump of her feet and feeling her heartbeat in time, her breathing relaxed. Rose's mind started to clear as she wondered back to the day Mary left for America. She remembered standing at the boarding gate smiling proudly beside Frank as they blew kisses to their only daughter. As Mary disappeared into the distance with the other passengers, she remembered the tug on her heartstrings, and even further back to when her little girl was thirteen years old.

Mary stood behind their bar in Tenerife with her sister Sheila, who was teaching her to mix cocktails. They were like a double act together, juggling and flicking bottles between each other while delighting the customers and Queens alike. The bar staff also loved having this cute little girl behind the bar because the tip jar would triple in size while she was working her magic. Then proudly she remembered Mary receiving her offer to attend Trinity College in pharmacy studies. They were so happy because she had studied and worked so hard for her exams. It was the perfect time for her to go to America with her school friend, June. Rose and Frank wanted her to spread her wings and experience life while she was young and carefree. She was so full of life, but innocent and wise at the same time. Rose knew in her heart that the two girls together would be fine and have a great adventure! When they chatted on the phone, Rose was happy for Mary that she had found a job at the college working as a mixologist and bar person. Mary would tell her excitedly about the friends she had met and about being able to use the college facilities, including the gym and swimming pool. She told her about meeting the handsome Brian and how he introduced her to his head coach Ed, who gave her the job, and how he was like a grandfather to her. It all sounded so perfect, and Rose would regale everyone in the Queen Vick about her adventures as they gathered around for the news. As the year went on, Mary got more attached to Brian, and they began dating. Mary sounded so happy, as was Rose, delighted for her daughter, who was now experiencing love for the first time. When they talked, Mary would babble on and on about how Brian did this, or Brian did that. She would tell of how they had won a big major game and claimed a big cup. Of course, Brian, being the captain, held it up for everyone to cheer. Mary was so excited and proud of him. As the months turned into a year, Rose was expecting Mary to start planning her return journey home and take up her studies again in Trinity. When she inquired about this, Mary would be evasive while changing the subject. Then Mary would suggest maybe postponing her course until a later date. It was obvious to Rose that she didn't want to leave Brian. Rose explained that Brian was also studying, and they could continue their relationship during their holidays. Mary countered that she would rather stay on another while. It was obvious Mary had made up her mind, and that particular call had ended badly. Later, when Rose would call Mary, she became even more evasive when Rose spoke about her coming home. After that, Rose heard from a friend that June had returned home to complete her studies. So, Rose made it her business to casually run into June while out shopping one day. She let on to be surprised to see her and invited her in for coffee to glean as much information as she could. June was genuinely glad to meet Rose. As they talked, Rose gradually began to include Mary in the conversation. As she did so, she noticed that June became a little nervous about how the conversation was going. Rose, seeing this, put June at her ease by saying,

"Wasn't Mary a gas character falling for Brian, and then staying on in America to be with her fella?"

At this, June relaxed a little and agreed with Rose. She let it slip that Brian had moved in with Mary and they were sharing the rent. It was then that June's eyes darkened, and Rose knew that she didn't want to continue talking about Mary and Brian getting together anymore. So, feeling the conversation had run its course, June finished her coffee in preparation to leave. As they parted, Rose felt a little guilty for catching her out. But as they said goodbye, she wondered had the girls fallen out with each other over Brian.? Over the next 18 months, the calls became less frequent as Mary and Brian continued their relationship. Mary became more distant and evasive until contact between them almost stopped unless Rose persisted in phoning her. Rose was worried sick about her child. She felt something was wrong; she was afraid to interfere in case Mary took a huff and cut her off altogether. She was having dreams where her mother would appear, looking sternly at her. She didn't know what to do; she had told both Sheila and Frank of her concerns, but they also were at a loss. Then, early this morning, Frank shook her awake, saying he was going to Brussels on a business trip. He told her his car wouldn't start and asked her for a lift to the airport. As Rose knew she had her spinning class booked for later, she put on her tracksuit and got her gym bag for showering. On the way to the airport with Frank, she realised she needed to use the loo. She parked up in the airport and said goodbye to Frank, then headed to the toilet. When she was finished and knew she had some time to spare, she decided to get herself a coffee. She could have picked any of about six coffee docks in the airport, but why she chose that one will never be known. Or maybe she did, as she could feel her mother's presence. It was then she saw Mary sitting there at the table like a lost child.

When she stopped for a breath in the park, she took out her phone and rang Sheila. She told her the whole story about meeting Mary and the dishevelled and distraught state she was in. She also said how relieved she was to have her home safe and sound. She finished by saying she would contact her again when she had more news of what had happened to her. She decided not to contact Frank just yet, as she knew he would be in meetings. She wanted time with Mary alone to find out what happened to her. How she ended up in Dublin airport in the state she was in, both mentally and physically, and what she could do to help her.

When she got back to the house, she checked on Mary, who was still fast asleep. It was late afternoon before she heard the water running for a bath. Rose started putting food together; she knew Mary would be famished by now. An hour later, Mary appeared at the kitchen door with a towel wrapped around her hair and wearing a dressing gown. When she saw her mother standing by the stove, she smiled at her, saying,

"Good morning, mum."

Rose smiled back before putting a big fry with a pot of tea down on the table. It was then that Mary knew she would have some explaining to do. She thought to herself,

"Where do I begin? And how much do I want to tell? Then she thought, I'll start from the beginning with the worst news.

So, Mary pronounced,

"Mum, I am pregnant, Brian is the father, and he doesn't know. I am never going back to America, and I have decided... I am keeping my baby."

Mary was trying to be strong as she looked at her mother with determination, but as she spoke, she just fell apart and broke down crying again. All Rose could do was to put her arms around her daughter and comfort her while saying,

"Let it out, take your time, your home now, home, safe and sound, with the support of your whole family."

As she comforted her, Rose's heart was breaking for her child as she watched her sobbing. Eventually, Mary regained her composure and began again slowly,

"Mum, oh mum, it was so wonderful in the beginning, and I was so happy at the college, I wanted to stay there forever with Brian".

Rose held Mary's hand in hers with a stern face and steely gaze as Mary began to tell her story.

10

As Mary started, she knew in her head; she would not be disclosing every detail of her relationship with Brian. Especially their most intimate ones of how she lost her virginity. But the thought of it brought back delightful, vivid memories that would still make her skin tingle. The first time was when Brian dropped her home at her flat one afternoon, loaded down with groceries, and he helped her carry them in. Mary already knew what was going to happen and longed for it. As they started putting their groceries away in the fridge, and with the area being so small, they turned together, almost touching. They could feel their very breaths; Brian gently put his arms around Mary's waist and drew her to him. As they gently kissed on the lips, Mary opened her mouth so they could explore each other with their tongues. As they kissed and caressed each other, Brian lifted Mary in his strong arms and carried her to the bed. Slowly, Mary started to open the buttons on her blouse.

Brian removed his shirt at the same time as Mary admired his pecks while opening her bra. They came together more passionately, kissing, probing, touching, caressing. When Brian entered Mary, she let out a soft groan. Brian stopped for a second, concerned, and he asked her if this was her first time. Smiling up at him, Mary nodded yes. Brian carried on making love to Mary ever so gently until they both climaxed together. Mary remembered when it was over, they lay in each other's arms, she felt so very safe and contented to be with such a beautiful man. She could feel the tears welling up in her eyes and her heart bursting with love for him. They made love two or three times again after that. Mary couldn't wait for his caring and gentle touch each time. Then she remembered back to the most exciting skin skin-tingling, erotic encounter they ever had.

Mary had been at work, and it had been a long day; the weather had been particularly warm and humid. Towards the end of her shift, a loud and boisterous group entered the bar, and Brian was among them. They all wanted instant service, and Mary tried to serve them as fast as she could. Some of the groups were moaning and complaining because they had to wait longer than expected. Brian stayed in the background, talking to the others as Mary cleared each customer one by one. She served the last girl her drink, a Hispanic girl, and Mary knew her as Marisol Mandez. She looked at Mary with hatred in her eyes. She told Mary to keep away from Brian or she would be sorry, then she picked up her drink and walked away. Mary didn't think much about her remark and just carried on working. She did remember that same girl in that group with Brian before.

When her shift was over, she looked over at the group. She could see Brian talking and laughing. Marisol had her arm around his waist. When their eyes met, she tightened her grip on Brian's waist while smirking at her. Mary felt the pangs of jealousy and anger as she left the building.

She was hot and clammy from the heat and decided to go for a swim as she often did after work. As she walked to the gym, Brian, like before, appeared behind her out of nowhere, frightening her. He wanted to know if they would meet up tomorrow on her day off. Mary was a little annoyed at the carry-on between Brian and Marisol in the bar, and she also told him about her warning to keep away from him. Brian just laughed at her unease, saying that she was like that with all the guys. He told Mary not to pay her any attention as "she", Mary, was his girl exclusively. Mary, feeling appeased at what Brian told her, smiled and agreed to meet tomorrow before kissing him on the lips. So, Mary carried on to the gym as Brian went back to his group.

Mary knew the gym closed at nine pm, and she had about an hour in the pool to herself doing lengths that she loved. After her swim, she got out of the pool totally refreshed and invigorated. While Mary showered alone in the ladies' dressing rooms, she washed the soap and suds from her clean hair as she hummed to herself. Suddenly, a hand touched her shoulder, and Mary's heart stopped with fright. Defensively, she turned to try and fend off whoever the attacker was in the shower with her. She could not believe her eyes when she saw it was Brian standing there, totally naked and smiling at her. She was just about to rebuke him, while closing her fists to pound them on his chest for giving her such a fright. But he gently pulled her into his chest, kissing her passionately on the mouth. Mary immediately melted into his touch and returned his kiss hungrily, forgetting all about their surroundings as they fondled and squirmed together in the soapy hot water, noisily drowning out Mary's moans of ecstasy. Brian effortlessly lifted her while Mary wrapped her legs around his waist, then he slowly lowered her down onto his manhood. When they were finished, Mary thought her heart would explode with excitement. She could feel the blood in her veins pumping through her body at such a rate she thought her head would explode. As she gasped for air, trying to fill her lungs, her whole body shuddered and shook. Brian gently stroked and kissed her until she gained her composure again.

When she looked up at him, she could see the love in his eyes, and Mary giggled as she lay into his chest, totally besotted. She stood there thinking of how daring he was to sneak into the ladies' dressing room unseen. This also proved his love for her after her encounter with Marisol in the bar. She knew for sure that she was his only love, and she, in turn, loved him deeply. When they had finished and it was time to leave the shower cubicle, Mary popped her head around the curtain to see if the coast was clear. Then she nodded at Brian with a wink, and he disappeared down the cubicles. As she watched his broad shoulders and tight little bum disappear around the corner, she smiled to herself at this sight.

Later, when Mary came out of the gym, she was disappointed that Brian was not waiting for her. She assumed that he had returned to his group and decided to make her own way home. On the journey home, she relived their encounter repeatedly, of what had happened in the shower room. Her body tingled, while her crotch area became moist from thinking about Brian and how bold and adventurous he was. She could not sleep that night with such erotic thoughts going through her head. Happily, she looked forward to seeing him again the next day. It was midday before Brian showed up. Mary had been waiting for him since early and was a little miffed when he did show up. After he came in, Mary faked her annoyance, pointing out the time he arrived. Brian smiled and said he was sorry for not coming earlier, but with a sly grin, he took from his pocket a gift box with a ribbon wrapped around it. He told her the reason he was late was because he had to pick up a present for her while handing Mary the box. Mary opened the box excitedly to reveal a golden bracelet with what looked like a cat dangling from the clasp. Mary was delighted with her gift but was somewhat confused as to what the cat meant. Brian explained that it was a Panther; he explained, it was the nickname his teammates had given him. His teammates said that, in the game, he could move swiftly and silently without being seen before making his strike. Mary pondered the little shiny golden trinket hanging from the chain, then agreed, mischievously saying,

"Was that how you moved last night, in the lady's shower room, just like a Panther. Swiftly and silently, without being seen?"

Brian laughed at this, and they kissed passionately before making love again.

Then Mary went back to telling her mother how things had changed for the worse.

11

Mary began telling Rose that it all went downhill when June, without warning, suddenly announced that she was going back to Ireland. It was two months before she was due to go home, and Mary was gutted.

"I couldn't believe it, we were like sisters, sharing makeup, clothes, and sometimes even underwear. We went to the best nightclubs, dancing, drinking, and looking out for each other. I even introduced her to loads of guys from the college football team, and we went on many double dates together."

June was dating Skip, a fullback on Brian's team, and when we went out, we would have such a good time. Whenever the guys were playing, we would get complimentary VIP tickets to see the game. And of course, this included free college team merchandise like jerseys, baseball caps, key rings, and complimentary food and drinks. We loved going to the games where we would be shouting from the sidelines for our team, then afterwards, meeting up with the guys for a good night out. Neither of us was ever involved with drugs, but around the campus, if you were in the market, and knew the right people, there was plenty available. It was on such a night, after a game, that we were in a nightclub having a good time. Brian and Skip were in high spirits, having won their game. June and I were dancing together on the floor and enjoying ourselves. While we were dancing, I glanced over at the boys who were laughing and joking. Then, I saw Skip pouring some white powder into both our drinks. At first, I thought I had imagined it, but I knew for sure when I walked off the floor and challenged Skip. He knew immediately he had been caught and tried to make light of it by saying,

" It was only an upper and I thought it would enhance your night."

Skip was laughing it off as Brian just sat there with a silly grin on his face. I was furious as June approached, and I told her what Skip did. Instantly, the night ended as June, and I grabbed our coats and bags to go home. The two guys stood up, holding out their arms apologetically, saying,

"Girls, it was only a harmless bit of fun; we are sorry."

Neither of us was listening as we left the nightclub and hailed a taxi before the guys could follow us. On the journey home, June started to cry while saying that she had really liked Skip but would never have anything to do with him again after what he tried tonight. I said that I didn't know what they were thinking of in attempting to spike our drinks. I was disgusted at Brian for letting Skip get away with it. After that night, June never had anything to do with Skip. Brian didn't show his face in the bar or contact me for weeks. Brian did appear again, out of nowhere, when Mary was least expecting it to frighten her. As he stood there with that silly grin on his face, he pulled from behind his back a big bunch of flowers. Mary was delighted to see him but didn't let on. Brian, while holding out the flowers, said how much he had missed her. Mary, aching for his touch, stood her ground. Brian said that he was very sorry for messing up and promised that something like that would never happen again. He continued that all he wanted to do was make it up to her if she would find it in her heart to forgive him. He knew when Mary relented as he threw his big arms around her in a bear hug.

June was happy for Mary getting back with Brian. She also admitted that she missed Skip. So, Mary made it known to Brian about June. On a sunny afternoon, the two girls received tickets to a football match, and they were delighted. At the game, they were sitting beside two handsome guys who started chatting them up. The girls were enamoured while flirting and laughing back with the guys. Then, from behind, another guy tapped one of the lads on the shoulder. He said that he should be careful, as she, meaning Mary, belonged to the Panther. The conversation stopped immediately as the guy beside Mary looked at the bracelet she was wearing. Mary was disgusted, realising what the bracelet meant. She felt it had ruined her day because she did not belong to anyone. Then she realised, when she thought back to any encounter she had with men. Once they saw her bracelet on her wrist, they usually backed away from her company. Mary immediately took the bracelet off and put it in her bag. When the match finished, she decided to go straight home instead of going back to the clubhouse. June went on to meet Skip.

As the year was coming to an end, the girls decided they would take their road trip as planned. It was a quiet day in the bar, and June had called for Mary to take her home when she had finished her shift. The girls had a map spread out on the bar and were talking about where they would go. As they were sipping their drinks and talking, a few customers came into the bar, and Brian was among them. When he saw their maps spread out, he wandered over. As Mary put up their order on the bar, he inquired as to where they had decided to go. Excitedly, the girls showed him the route they were going to take. Their journey would take them down along the coast towards Mexico. Stopping off along the way at Huntington Beach, Juan Capistrano, San Diego, and then Tijuana, staying at Rivera Beach. When Brian saw where the girls were taking their road trip, his eyes lit up. He told them that he and Skip had made that very same journey many times and had a blast. He said that if it wasn't crowding their style, and if the girls were interested, that maybe the four of them could meet up towards the end of their trip at Mission Beach, San Diego boardwalk. He continued that there was an excellent motel they always stayed in, and it had a lovely pool with great food. Both girls were delighted with his suggestion and agreed to meet them in Huntington. A few days later, Mary and June set off on their adventure, heading south along the West Coast of California, singing and bopping as they drove. They loved the journey down the coast, stopping off wherever they liked for food or swimming. Each night, they would park up in a motel, then get dressed and go out drinking and dancing. When they crossed into Mexico at Tijuana, they were so relaxed and enjoying their holiday together. They checked into a beautiful hotel on the Riviera and went swimming and surfing. That evening, they sat together at a spectacular beach club, sipping cocktails while listening to the mariachi bands singing traditional Mexican songs. Mary thought she was in heaven as the gentle breeze softly brushed her hair while they watched a stunning sunset. It was then she thought of Brian and how romantic it would be if he were here also. Her thoughts were broken as the mariachis approached their table to serenade the girls. They laughed and enjoyed their singing as they tipped their glasses together and drank their cocktails. After a couple of fantastic days, the girls were spending their last night by the beach club, sipping cocktails. Suddenly, in his usual way of appearing out of nowhere, Brian turned up, totally surprising Mary. Standing beside her, he asked if she would like to dance. Mary was dumbfounded but delighted to see him as she jumped up and threw her arms around him. Then she looked over his shoulder, and she saw Skip approaching with a smile on his face also. Mary and June made room for the boys to sit beside them as they asked what they were doing there. The boys answered that they knew where they were staying and took a chance that they might be at the bar. The whole night became magical as the four friends talked, laughed, drank, and danced the last night away. That night, Mary and Brian slept in the girls' room, while June and Skip slept in the boys' room. The next morning, when it was time to check out, the girls were still packing as the boys pulled up outside their room. Skip came in holding his gym bag over his shoulder, inquiring if they were ready to head back. It was obvious they were not. So, Skip suggested that the boys head on up the coast to San Diego and meet them there; everyone agreed. Before he left, Skip asked if he could use their toilet before heading off. The girls just waved him away as they were busy packing their bags. Skip dropped his bag on the bed while going into the bathroom, which fell to the floor. When he had finished, Skip ran out and jumped in the car, waving at the girls while beeping the horn as they drove away. When the girls were packed up and ready to leave, they realised that Skip had forgotten his gym bag. Not thinking anything about it, they threw it in the boot of their own car with their luggage to return it to him later. As they reached the border at Tijuana, ready to cross over into the USA, the girls chatted casually together. They spoke about the fabulous hotel they had stayed in and how they had spent their last night making love, which topped off their road trip. In line, bit by bit, they approached the border guards. They had their passports ready for inspection and were very relaxed as they edged up to the inspection booth. Just then dogs started barking at a car in front of them. A guy jumped out of his car and started to run away, causing a big commotion. The girls watching all this got frightened to see the guards drawing their weapons to apprehend the culprit. As the distracted guards apprehended the guy who was running away, another guard stepped into the booth and asked them to produce their passports. He asked them about their business for visiting Mexico. The girls explained that they were on a road trip and were returning after their holiday. Without showing any emotion while keeping an eye on his colleagues, apprehending the running guy. He stamped their passports and roughly told them to move on. The girls immediately did as they were ordered, but were still a little frightened at their ordeal crossing back over the border.

When the girls reached San Diego, they were back in good spirits again after their ordeal at the border. They regaled the boys about the running guy and the serious faces and attitude of the border guards. They all spent the rest of the day swimming and surfing. Mary couldn't remember having had such a good time, but the next day, when they all left San Diego, June's demeanour changed. On the drive home, she became silent and serious as she drove. Mary could feel the tension; she asked June if she had a row with Skip? She also inquired if she was, OK? When June turned to face Mary, she could see tears rolling down her cheeks, and she was crying.

Mary instructed June to pull into a roadhouse to have coffee. When they were inside, Mary seated June in a booth and ordered coffee and muffins. She then sat down in front of June while taking both her hands in hers and asking what had happened. June was distraught when she started to tell her what had happened. When she spoke, Mary couldn't believe what she was saying. June told Mary that after their reunion with Brian and Skip the evening before, when they reached San Diego, the boys were waiting. After they checked in for the night, they all went swimming together. It was a fantastic fun fun-filled day. That evening, in the hotel room, June noticed Skip slipping out of bed, thinking she was asleep. Then he went to her clutch bag like he was searching for something and found what he was looking for. June was suspicious of his behaviour and waited for him to leave the bedroom. She then got up quietly and watched from the window as Skip opened her car trunk and retrieved his gym bag. He then returned to the hotel room. June was already back in bed pretending to be asleep while Skip put the key back in her bag. When she heard Skip going into the shower room and turning on the water, she got up again and went to the closet where

Skip had hidden his bag. She opened it to see what was inside, and she couldn't believe her eyes to see a whole bag of tablets and pills of every kind.

Mary couldn't believe what she was hearing. She asked herself, "Could this be true?" Then it dawned on her, was Brian also involved in drugs? Would they do such a thing to turn the girls into drug mules? Knowing what would happen to them if they were stopped at the border. Did they care that little about them that they would leave them to their fate in Mexico? They could have been locked up for years. As Mary consoled her friend, she couldn't speak. The realisation of what had happened, and what could have happened, hit home. She thought to herself, how lucky they were that the border guards didn't stop them because of the running guy. She felt her stomach churn at the thought of the consequences of being branded a drug runner. It was a long time before either girl spoke as they sat and stared out the window of the Roadhouse. Suddenly, her phone rang, breaking the silence and making them jump. Mary looked at the screen to see Brian's name. She composed herself before answering. Brian said they were almost home and wanted to know how far they were behind them.

Smiling weakly, Mary said that they had stopped for a bite to eat and to continue their own journey home. She said that they would go home themselves and catch up tomorrow. Brian seemed happy enough with her answer and said, "OK, I love you," before hanging up. Then Mary turned her phone off before silently returning it to her bag.

When they got back, the atmosphere had changed between the girls; their trip to Mexico was never mentioned again, and they just went back to work. They both had spoken about reporting what had happened to the police. But if they did, would they be believed that they were not part of the scheme to smuggle the drugs? So, they agreed as the trip was coming to a natural end, it was best to let sleeping dogs lie.

12

A few days later, Mary was at work when Brian came in alone. He sat up at the bar and ordered juice. Mary, giving him the cold shoulder, served him but carried on working. Brian, feeling the tension between them, was looking confused as to what had happened after they had split up in San Diego. He thought everything was OK between them. As she passed by, he put out his hand and caught her wrist, asking what was wrong. Mary snapped her wrist away, saying,

"You know very well what is wrong."

Brian, still looking confused, shrugged his shoulders at what she was talking about, but Mary kept on working and didn't answer him. Just then, all his friends came into the bar and joined him, so the conversation could not continue. Afterwards, when Mary was heading to the swimming pool, like before, Brian appeared out of nowhere. Mary jumped to see him beside her, but kept walking. Brian followed while asking the question,

"What was wrong? What did I do, or not do something I should have done?"

Mary was furious at this stage; she swung round to face him. She was spitting venom as she told him about the despicable trick he had played on them in Mexico. Brian stood there motionless, listening as Mary told him about the bag of drugs. When she had finished, she stormed away before Brian could defend himself, leaving him standing on the curb. As Mary stormed away and knew that Brian wasn't following her, she let her emotions flow and cried. While she was swimming, with each stroke she took in the pool, she pounded so hard with each breath she took in and let out. She cried until she could cry no more tears. She had pounded him out of her system, then she thought to herself, "Maybe it was time to go home after all."

That night in the flat, Mary announced to June that she intended to book a flight home with her. June was silent for a moment before answering. Then she turned over to face Mary with a look of sadness on her face. She said that Mary's decision must have been very hard to make, as she knew how very much in love she was with Brian. But given that the boys were mixed up in drug running and not even caring what would have happened to them at the border. She felt Mary had made the right choice in breaking all ties with Brian. Mary didn't answer June as she spoke. She just lay on her side, facing away from June and letting her tears flow onto her pillow, until sleep drifted over her broken heart.

13

The next day, while at work, Ed came in all harassed as usual, holding his satchel. It was loaded down with plans of game connotations, with players' names and positions in his hands. Mary tried to have a word with him. But as there was a big game coming up that weekend, he didn't want to be distracted from his task of picking a team. So, Mary went back to work, at the same time, keeping an eye on him as he worked. From time to time, she would bring coffee to his favourite booth. But Ed was so engrossed in his work, he didn't even notice, or if he did, he would grunt a quick thank you. He had made it evident that he didn't want to be disturbed. By late afternoon, Ed looked a little more relaxed as he had decided how the game would be played and who was to be in the lineout. As he sat back and rubbed his tired neck with his big hands, he stretched out his arms above his head and breathed out a sigh of relief. Mary was watching him and knew that this was her chance to talk to him. She brought a big mug of steaming coffee and a freshly made sandwich to the table. Ed, looking up, surprised but happy to see the food as he hadn't eaten all day, said,

"Some guy would be fortunate to have you as his girl."

Mary smiled back, saying,

"I thought that you would be needing this about now."

While looking down at the sandwich.

Ed, feeling the pangs of hunger, picked up the sandwich as Mary asked if she could have a quiet word with him. Ed, with his mouth full of the first bite of his sandwich, moved some of his paperwork aside so Mary could sit beside him. Then he turned and gave her his full attention, waiting for what she was going to say. Moments passed as Ed chewed, waiting, but Mary sat beside him with her head bowed. When she finally looked up to face Ed, he could see that she was very distraught. Ed stopped chewing and swallowed hard to be able to speak to Mary. Very concerned, he took her hand in his, saying,

"Oh, my dear, whatever is the problem?"

But Mary's tears continued to flow, and Ed waited for her to compose herself. When she eventually did speak, she looked into Ed's eyes, saying,

"Ed, I'm very sorry, but I am giving you my notice and I will be returning to Ireland."

She waited for Ed's reply. The look on Ed's face changed from great concern to anger and then to great joy. With a big smile on his face, he grabbed Mary by the shoulders and pulled her into him, giving her a big hug, he said,

"Oh, thank God, I thought you were going to tell me something terrible had happened to you."

Mary pulled back to face him and asked,

"Are you not disappointed I'm leaving?"

Ed tut-tutted her, saying,

"You are indeed one of our best barmaids, and you would be dearly missed."

Then he continued softly,

"You came to America for an adventure and to see some of the world. But now, it was time to return home to continue your studies."

He continued,

"Anyway, if you felt you would want to return next year, the door would always be open."

On hearing Ed's words, Mary put her arms around his neck and gave him a big hug back. As they hugged, suddenly Ed pulled away to look at Mary. He had that look of concern on his face again as he asked her,

"Does Brian know anything of your plans"?

Mary shook her head sadly, saying that they had split up. Relieved, Ed said that it might be the best thing for her not to let him know. Mary was confused as to why Ed would say this, but decided to let it go as she had no intention of speaking to Brian ever again. But still, as Mary thought of Brian, her heart would ache for him, and her eyes would fill up at the thought of leaving him forever.

14

A few days before they were to return to Ireland, Mary was putting together the last few things for our journey home. June was at work finishing out her notice. When Mary had finished packing, she put away her case and decided to take a shower. Afterwards, when she came out with a towel wrapped around her head, she got an awful shock to see Brian sitting at the end of her bed. She spat out the question,

"How did you get in here?"

Brian didn't answer her; he just sat there with his head bent, looking down at his feet. Mary stood by the shower room door waiting for an answer, but Brian just sat there not saying a word for what seemed like minutes. When he eventually broke the silence, his voice was low and sorrowful. He never lifted his head as he spoke; he just kept looking at his shoes. As Mary watched, she could see big wet tears fall from his eyes, then he began,

"I found out why you are leaving me, and if I were in your place, I would do the same. But before you go, I wanted you to know that I was an innocent victim in all this, as you and June were. I thought Skip was my friend, but I was wrong. If I had known what he was up to, I would never have let it happen. I couldn't believe he would do such a thing."

When Brian had finished talking, he slowly stood up, looking like a defeated man. He looked sadly across at Mary, saying,

"If ever you could find it in your heart to forgive me for not protecting you, you could contact me. I would meet you anywhere in the world you choose. I love you, Mary, and would go to the end of the earth for you in a heartbeat."

Before Mary could reply, he turned and let himself out, leaving her dumbstruck and wide-eyed. Over the next few days, Mary was perplexed; she couldn't sleep, and she told June about what had transpired between Brian and her. She tried to reason with herself over and over, how she should break all ties with Brian? But her heart was breaking at the thought of leaving the love of her life. She also felt that she was making the biggest mistake of her life. Her brain wouldn't let her rest, but what was she to do? On that day they were to leave, Mary stopped in her tracks in the LAX airport Terminal. As June turned to face her, still holding her trolley full of luggage, she already knew what Mary was about to say. Before Mary could speak, June looked at her pleadingly, saying,

"Please, Mary, don't do this. He is not the sort of man you think he is."

But Mary stood her ground, saying,

"June, I believe him, I've thought it over, and in my heart, I know he wouldn't have done this to us."

At this stage, June was beginning to lose her patience, but she pleaded again with Mary, saying,

"Look, Mary, why not board the plane now, and when you get home, you can make contact with Brian again after you have time to think?"

But Mary still stood her ground as June tried again to reason with her, saying,

"Mary, I didn't want to tell you this, but the last time Brian was home in Ireland, it was to defend himself against a rape charge."

At hearing this, Mary was shocked with a look of disbelief on her face. June continued that she had found out through a friend from Donegal. She said that Brian had raped a girl in the showroom of the local swimming pool. But the girl later withdrew the charge when Brian returned to defend himself. Everyone believed the girl, because they knew that Brian had intimidated her. It was because he had tried to do the same thing previously, to another girl. Mary recalled back to her beautiful experience with Brian in the shower when he appeared naked out of nowhere. She couldn't believe that such a wonderful moment could be marred by such a disgusting remark that June had made could be true. So, Mary retaliated with tears in her eyes, saying,

"I don't believe you."

But June continued,

"Why would I say such a thing if it wasn't true? "

Very angry at this stage, Mary said,

"Because you just want me to go home with you now."

June had had enough and lost her patience again with Mary, saying,

"Look, Mary, I'm getting on this plane now to go home. I have given you the facts; I really didn't want to tell you this. But if you stay, I think you will regret it for the rest of your life. I think Brian is a liar, a cheat, and he is manipulating you. I also think that the tears he shed in the flat were only crocodile tears."

Mary said to June,

"She didn't believe her, and it was a nasty trick to pull on her to make her board the plane."

June had heard enough, saying,

"Well, you do what you want with the information I have given you."

Then, June angrily turned away, pushing her trolley towards the check-in desk, leaving Mary behind. That was the last time they spoke.

15

Rose never spoke or showed any emotion while Mary told her story. She just sat encouragingly beside her, topping up her tea from time to time.

"Mom, oh mom, how could I have been so naive, so blind, so stupid. I let my best friend go home without me knowing that she was telling the truth. But I was just too stubborn and thick to listen to her."

Mary continued, that day, I got back to our flat knowing our lease was up within two days and I would have nowhere to stay. I don't know what I was thinking; all I could think about was falling into the arms of Brian. As soon as I got home, I called Brian and told him that I had decided to stay. He whooped and hollered on the phone before telling me he would be over within the hour. My heart was pounding when I saw his car arrive outside. I couldn't contain myself when he walked through the door with a big smile on his face. Immediately, we lunged into each other's arms and made love all afternoon and night. When we had our fill of lovemaking, we lay back on the bed, totally exhausted. I told Brian the situation I was in as to having nowhere to stay. He just laughed it off, saying that now I was his, we would get a place of our own. I couldn't believe the beautiful apartment he found for us off campus, and not too far from my work. It was so modern, with floor-to-ceiling windows looking out over a lovely park. The double bedroom had an ensuite with a rain shower and a dressing room off to the side, and the sitting room had white Italian leather seating with a wraparound bar area. It also had a fully fitted kitchen with all mod cons. Everything was new and plush, and it even had a wall safe. When I asked Brian how we could afford such a place, he laughed it off, saying that it was a college perk for only the best football players.

I thought I was in heaven when he hugged me and then carried me to the bedroom. Ed was genuinely delighted to see me back with big hugs and kisses. Everything seemed to fit back in place, and Mary couldn't believe her luck with the way things were working out, work-wise, and accommodation-wise. When Mary said to Ed about how happy she was to be staying in such a beautiful apartment, that was a college perk for the players. Ed looked a little confused but didn't elaborate on what Mary had told him. So, Mary let the subject drop, thinking that maybe the college did not want to advertise the fact that they were giving out perks to football players. The only person who wasn't happy to see her back was Marisol, the Hispanic girl. As usual, when she came to the bar for a drink, Mary could see the venom and hatred in her eyes. When she was served, she picked up her drink, then, looking at Mary, she said,

"I warned you to keep away from him, but you wouldn't listen. So, anything that happens from now on, you've brought it on yourself, little virgin. If you think moving in with him will save you, you will find out you are gravely mistaken."

Then Marisol stormed away from the counter, leaving Mary in no doubt she had meant what she had said. For the first time since Mary arrived in America, she felt afraid. She knew Marisol had a violent reputation and was involved with drugs and the people who dealt in them.

On a dark, chilly evening within a month of Mary being threatened, she had finished her shift and was heading to the pool for a well-deserved swim. As she approached the complex, a group of girls were gathered on her route, and Mary would have to pass them. Mary was not paying much attention to the group as she passed. Suddenly, out of the blue, she was punched on the side of her head, which knocked her sideways. The shock of the punch disoriented her as she staggered. Before she could gather herself, she felt another blow to the other side of her face that made her fall to the ground. Immediately, Mary wrapped herself into a ball to try and protect herself as her attacker, or attackers, kicked her repeatedly. The violence of the attack was unrelenting as Mary was kicked from head to toe repeatedly. As she began to lose consciousness, she heard a car beeping its horn, and the beating stopped. Her attackers then disappeared, but before they left, one person whispered in her ear, saying,

"You were lucky this time, little virgin, but I'm not finished yet; we will dance again."

Then Mary passed out. When she regained consciousness, she was in the campus Medical Centre. Feeling sore and uncomfortable, she looked around to see a nurse with her back to her. She asked the nurse where she was, and the nurse turned to face Mary with a smile. She told her that she would have swelling and bruises for a while, but she was a lucky girl, as no permanent damage was done in the attack. The nurse asked if she was feeling up to it, and a police officer was waiting outside to interview her. Mary tried to lift her head but was feeling woozy as she lay back down again. After a few seconds, she asked the nurse if anyone had been contacted. The nurse answered that her father was waiting outside. Mary looked at the nurse quizzingly, and she smiled at her, saying,

"Don't worry, it's only Ed the football coach, he's like a father to everyone. But to get in to see you, he had to say he was family."

Immediately, Mary asked if she could see him, and the nurse agreed. When Ed came into the room, the look of shock on his face said it all, and Mary started to cry. Ed raced to comfort Mary by wrapping his arms around her. When Mary regained her composure, Ed asked if she could identify any of her attackers. Mary remembered the words whispered in her ear, but couldn't determine if it was Marisol or not, as she hadn't seen anyone because it happened so quickly. Ed was so kind to Mary. He stayed with her until Brian arrived many hours later. When he came into the room, Mary noticed that there was tension between the two men. She pushed it away, thinking that it must have been the state she was in that caused it. When Ed left, Brian was angry; he wanted the names of those who did this to her. Mary could see in his eyes the danger she could put a person into if she gave him a name. But in all honesty, she didn't see her attackers, so there was no point in naming anyone, even if she did have her own suspicions. Muggings on the campus were very rare, and word went around like wildfire. Students were nervous to walk alone until the culprits were apprehended. Later that day, Mary was discharged with plenty of painkillers for her cracked ribs and sore neck. When she saw her face in the mirror, she could have cried. The side of her eye was swollen and black and blue. Her nose was plastered, and her bottom lip was split and swollen, too. She felt it was hard to sit up, lie down, or even take in a deep breath without being in pain.

16

Ed, being the gentleman he was, called around every day. Sometimes he would bring a bunch of flowers, chocolates, or a small basket of fruit. When Brian came back, she could see that this annoyed him as he banged around the kitchen. He asked if Ed had taken a fancy to her? Mary laughed this off, saying that he was like a father to her, and she was happy to be paid while she was off work. Brian just grunted and walked away. This disturbed Mary a little because Brian always looked up to Ed respectfully. It was a further two weeks before Mary returned to work. On her first day back, Brian insisted on driving Mary to the campus. Before she got out of the car, Mary leaned over to kiss Brian goodbye. As she did so, he caught her by the wrist, holding her tightly. When their eyes met, he looked at her earnestly, saying,

"Put this back on your wrist and wear it always, as it will keep you safe."

When Mary looked down at his open hand, she could see the gold chain with the little Panther attached. Mary didn't want to argue, as Brian had been very kind to her during her convalescence. So, she smiled at him and put it on while he watched. This seemed to have pleased him; he smiled back before saying,

"Promise me, you will wear it always?"

Mary just smiled back, nodding her head in agreement before getting out of the car. Mary felt great to be back at work after the confines of the apartment. When she finished her shifts, she would go for a swim. Always, when she came out of the pool, Brian would be waiting to drive her home. This would bother her a little as she felt that Brian had taken over the role of her protector. When he picked her up, he would always kiss her on the cheek while checking she was wearing her bracelet. Then, on seeing she was wearing it, he would smile at her and drive home. After about six months of this, Mary had had enough of being minded. So, not to offend Brian, she decided to take up jogging and told him that she felt safe again. Mary would jog home after her swim, saying to Brian that she wanted to keep her figure; Brian was a little perturbed at this but grunted his approval. Besides, it was getting to the gaming season, and he had to attend many training sessions. Also, from time to time, he would have to go away for weekend training sessions, and Mary enjoyed the alone time. When he returned from those weekends, he was always upbeat and hyper. He would become very animated when making love, not lovingly and gently as Mary liked. But she couldn't complain as he got extra payments for those training sessions. Then he would take her out to expensive restaurants and nightclubs afterwards. One night, in one of the clubs, Mary saw Skip with a group of people across the dance floor.

Mary shuddered when she saw Marisol in his company. As she watched, to her horror, she saw Brian, who was coming back from the bar, stop at their table. They all hugged, slapped hands, and joked with each other, laughing out loud. Mary was even more horrified when Brian hugged Marisol before heading back to their table. When he had left them, Marisol looked across at Mary, and their eyes met. With a jeering grin on her face, she lifted her hand, making the silhouette of a gun. She then pointed it at Mary and closed her thumb like she was firing it at her. When Brian reached her table, Mary stood up angrily, saying that they were leaving. Brian looked confused as Mary brushed her way through the crowd towards the door. Mary was shaking in the car on the way home. Brian could sense her anger and asked what had happened in the club. Mary swung around to face Brian and said,

"You know very well what happened, talking to those people and especially Marisol, whom you kissed."

Brian said that it is just as well to stay friendly with them and not to make enemies, then he continued,

"And besides, I have to play football with Skip because he's on my team."

"Oh, for God's sake, Mary retorted, but not Marisol, she's not on your team". Brian answered,

"Ah, she is harmless and just likes to hang out with the team to be seen".

But this made Mary even angrier, as she blurted out,

"She is not that harmless, because I think it was, she who attacked me for being with you."

At this, Brian immediately stepped on the brake pedal hard while pulling into the curb. The cars behind had to swerve to avoid him. Brian turned to face her, and she could see the anger and danger in his eyes. She knew she shouldn't have said anything, but she was angry, too. With the engine ticking over, Brian was staring at her. He waited for her to elaborate on what she had said. Mary took a deep breath before telling Brian about what was whispered in her ear and why she thought it was Marisol. Then she told Brian about the nightclub and Marisol making the silhouette of a gun, then pulling the trigger. When she was finished, Brian sat beside her silently, thinking. Mary wasn't sure if he believed her or not; she waited for his reaction. Finally, as if he had made his decision, he turned to her and spoke,

"OK, leave it with me, and I will deal with Marisol myself."

Before Mary could ask him what he meant by that statement, Brian put the car back into gear again and pulled out dangerously onto that road while cars beeped and swerved again. They drove home and went to bed that night in total silence. Marisol, or what happened that night, was never mentioned again. It was about six weeks later, Brian came home from a training session, or so he told her, that was where he was. He seemed very quiet and distracted. At dinner, Mary asked him if everything was OK. Brian was miles away, and Mary had to ask him a second time. When she eventually interrupted his thoughts, he just grunted that he was fine. But Mary knew something was wrong, and he was not telling her. A few days later, while Mary was at work, word started to filter through that Marisol was found dead from an apparent drug overdose. Mary felt awful when she heard the news. She suspected Brian was involved, but chastised herself, asking why she would think such a terrible thing?

17

Word got back that Marisol was found with an injection still stuck in her arm. There was no evidence of foul play, so no investigation was made into her death. After that, Brian became increasingly paranoid. One evening, he came home in a terrible mood, having been left on the bench during a football match. His lovemaking became even more aggressive until it got to the stage that Mary was trying to avoid him. And when she was out shopping, she would feel someone was watching her. When she turned around, as usual, nobody was there. But later, somehow Brian would appear out of nowhere. Mary thought to herself, maybe I'm becoming paranoid, also, but still, the feeling never went away. It was then that she started checking her reflection in the windows and mirrors of cars, etc. And sure enough, she caught Brian watching her. He was across the street, hiding at a corner shop when he should have been training.

When she turned around, he had disappeared. After Mary got home that evening, she never mentioned a thing, but from then on, she would always check behind herself to see who was watching or following. She casually let it drop into their conversation that she thought she saw Brian in his car while she was shopping. Brian grunted that it couldn't have been his car, as he was at the pitch training all day. Mary knowingly let the subject drop. Afterwards, Mary noticed that Brian's football training weekends had come to a halt, and so did expensive dinners and nights out at the clubs. It was obvious money was starting to get tight.

To try and help out, Mary suggested to Brian that she had savings if he was short for their rent. Brian became very aggressive while shouting at Mary that if he needed money, he could get plenty. Then he stormed away, slamming the door behind him, leaving Mary very worried. Mary was at her wits' end; she didn't know who to turn to. One evening, when Ed was in the lounge studying his sheets and match permutations, Mary approached him. Just like the gentleman he was, Ed pushed aside his paperwork so Mary could sit beside him.

Ed could see the worried look on her face, so to lighten the mood, he said to her,

"Whatever is troubling you, it cannot be as bad as it seems right now."

Ed took both Mary's hands in his, then looking into her eyes, he gently asked",

"How can I help you, darling?"

Mary explained about Brian's mood swings and the fact that he didn't seem to be training or playing as many games lately. Ed listened as Mary spoke, showing empathy as he nodded his head sorrowfully. When she had finished speaking. Ed waited for a moment, thinking about what he was going to say, then he began,

"Look, Mary, you are a very beautiful, intelligent girl, and I wouldn't hurt you for the world. What advice I am about to give you now would be the very same advice I would give to my own daughter."

Mary was horrified when Ed spoke. He told her that Brian had been dropped from the football program. Also, that he would try and manipulate every situation to his own advantage. He didn't care about the consequences or the fallout to anyone else once he got his own way. And it was everyone's fault but his when something went wrong. Ed told her that he was in no doubt that Brian was dabbling in drugs. He finished by saying that Brian's scholarship was before the board with a view to it being rescinded. Then Ed looked at Mary earnestly, saying that she should take his advice and cut and run while she could. He continued, Brian was on a downward spiral and could take her down with him if she stayed. When he had finished, Mary thanked Ed for his candidness and honest advice. Before leaving the table, she leaned over and kissed him on the cheek, then she sadly went back to work. Mary's heart was breaking. How could she leave the only man she'd ever loved? How could she desert him at a time he needed her most? She had to help him turn his life around. Then she pondered the question. How can I help him, and would I be strong enough to fix this? With more resilience, she thought to herself, I will give it my best shot, knowing she could never leave him.

18

That evening, Mary prepared a nice meal with candles and wine glasses on the table. Then she went to the wall safe and took out all her savings, which amounted to a considerable sum and laid it on the table. When Brian came in, he looked around the room, then, seeing the money on the table, he asked,

"What is this? Have we won the lottery?"

Smiling, Mary took Brian by the hand, saying,

"All in good time."

She sat him down at the table, and she then poured him a big glass of wine before retreating to the kitchen. His favourite, steak, onions, mushrooms, and mashed potatoes with gravy, was laid before him. Brian wolfed down the meal as Mary watched him, smiling and eating hers also. When he was finished, he sat back in his chair holding his tummy in satisfaction, exclaiming that he couldn't eat another bite. Mary, feeling very pleased that everything was going so well, started to tell Brian what the evening was about. She stood up and walked to the other side of the table, then, bending over Brian, she kissed him on the lips. Brian was sheepishly smiling up at her with a little boyish look on his face. Mary just wanted to take him in her arms and kiss him forever when he looked at her that way. Then she stood beside him, reaching across the table and taking the pile of dollars, she placed it in front of him, saying triumphantly,

"All of this is yours, my darling, every penny."

Confused, Brian looked up at Mary, so she pulled over another chair and sat beside him. She gently took his hands in hers, then, looking into his eyes, she said,

"I know you have been going through a rough patch with your academics and football. But I want you to know, my darling, that I am here for you one hundred per cent, always. And whatever I have is yours, as I am."

Mary waited expectantly, waiting for Brian to tell her his worries so she could take him in her arms and dissolve all his troubles. Together as an unbeatable team, they could take on the whole world if they had to. There was silence in the room for what seemed like minutes while Brian thought about what Mary had told him. Suddenly, like an explosion, Brian stood up. He then upended the table, glasses, plates, and cutlery, went flying across the floor. Mary jumped back in fright wide-eyed and looked at Brian. Brian turned to look at Mary, and she saw a terrible thing in his eyes that she had never seen before. He approached her in two steps, grabbing her by the shoulders, lifting her from the chair. She could feel a fear engulf her like a sword piercing her heart, then he shouted at her,

"Who the fuck have you been talking to? Was it that fucking old man?"

Before Mary could answer or reason with him, he punched her in the solar plexus, knocking the wind out of her, and she fell to the floor gasping for air. Holding her tummy in pain as she lay on the floor, she felt a warm liquid splashing over her face and hair. When she looked up to see what it was, she couldn't believe to see Brian urinating on top of her like an animal marking its territory. Mary just covered her head until he was finished. When it was all over, Brian stormed out of their apartment, leaving Mary on the floor sobbing and still gasping for air. After an hour of lying on the floor, Mary decided to get up, clean up, and have a shower. While she was showering, Brian slipped in behind her naked. Mary stopped washing her hair in shock, waiting for another onslaught of abuse. But Brian's voice behind her was soft and gentle as he put his strong arms around her, saying,

"I am so sorry, honey, I know now you were only trying to help me, and I acted terribly. I don't want to lose you and have decided I am going to try and fix things, to get us back on track, so to speak. Can you ever forgive me for the way I've acted?"

As he slowly and gently caressed her, Mary's heart melted. Of course, she forgave him immediately as she turned to face him, laying into his chest, then they made love. After the row, Brian was in a more upbeat mood, and Mary felt that things were looking up at last. A few weeks later, to Mary's delight, Brian said that he had organised a trip down the coast. He told her to pack a bag with swimming gear, a skimpy dress, and her passport. All week long, while at work, Mary looked forward to surfing and swimming in the sunshine. When the day finally arrived, Mary couldn't contain herself when she jumped into the front seat of the car. But Brian told her to climb into the back seat as they had a passenger to pick up. Confused, Mary did as she was told until she saw who the passenger was. When Brian pulled into that curb, popping the trunk for extra baggage. Skip walked around to the front passenger seat; he smiled at Mary getting in, but never said a word. On the drive down the coast, nothing was said until they reached the border at Tijuana. Brian turned to Mary, saying to show her passport and say you are a tourist visiting for a couple of days. Mary's heart was thumping because she knew something wasn't right about this trip and was too afraid to ask. When they got through the border, Brian drove into a shady area in Tijuana before pulling into what looked like a tyre fitting depot. As they pulled into the garage, the door was closed behind them. Then Brian spoke,

"OK, this is it, get your gear out of the trunk and let's go."

Immediately, they got out of the car and went outside with their luggage, where a limousine was waiting for them. They were driven to a roadside motel and left at the reception. Nothing was said to the receptionist as they signed the guest book. Then they walked around to their rooms, which were on the first floor. At the bottom of the stairs was a goon holding an automatic pistol. Without saying a word, he frisked Skip and Brian, then told Mary to hold her arms out and frisked her also. When he was satisfied that they weren't carrying any weapons, he nodded for them to proceed upstairs. On the top floor, there was another goon covering the guy below. He stood back and let them pass to their rooms. Skips' room was 107, and theirs was 109, adjacent to each other. Mary's heart was racing, and she was shaking as they closed the door to their room. Immediately, she rounded on Brian, asking,

"What the hell is going on?"

Brian answered,

"What do you mean? What's going on? I already told you I was going to get us back on track, and that's what you wanted, wasn't it?"

Mary couldn't believe what she was hearing; she thought she was going mad.

"I thought we were going away for the weekend together to fix things up between us, so what's Skip doing here?"

Brian said,

" He's part of our team to do business."

Then Mary remembered Skip putting the tablets in their car last time and said to Brian,

"But you promised me that you had nothing to do with Skip and the tablets last time,"

Brian answered,

"And I meant every word I said. I didn't know Skip had made a private deal when we were last here. Everything I told you was the truth."

Mary couldn't believe what Brian was saying, so she asked the question outright,

"Are we here dealing in drugs? Is this what we have lowered ourselves to now ... drug running?"

Brian just laughed at her and asked,

" Are you really that naive that you think we are here for anything else?"

Mary started to panic, she was shouting out loud,

"I want to go home; I want to go home now."

Suddenly, Brian grabbed her by the throat, saying threateningly,

"Listen, Mary, we are here now to do a bit of business. You were brought in because Marisol was removed from the team because of you. Now, you have a job to do; you don't mess these guys around. We are safe here; that is why the men with the guns are outside, for our protection. So, follow my lead and we will all come out of this smiling; if not, it could be a different scenario."

When Brian had finished speaking, he released his grip so Mary could catch her breath. Mary knew then the danger she was in, so she decided to play along, especially now that she knew what had happened to Marisol. That evening, Brian told Mary to wear a sassy dress and be prepared to do her thing as a mixologist if asked. He told her she would be meeting very important people tonight, so to play her role well. When they were ready to go, Brian nodded his approval when Mary emerged wearing a black skimpy mini dress, accentuating every curve of her body. So, the three of them headed out by limousine to a local nightclub in an upmarket area. When they were in the car, Brian whispered in her ear,

"Whatever you do tonight, make sure you leave your bracelet on your wrist at all times."

She didn't answer him but wondered what he meant by that statement. When they reached the nightclub, the lights in the area were blinding. There was a long queue outside with bouncers in black tuxedos standing behind a red rope, letting people enter one by one. As soon as they arrived, the rope was lifted, and they were escorted inside by a beautiful, smiling front-of-house lady. Then they were directed away from the main dancing area to a private section that was cordoned off. Even though the area was luxurious and plush, Mary felt it was sleazy. It was full of mostly young and middle-aged men dripping in gold chains, rings, and fancy watches. Scantily clad young girls were flaunting themselves as they served drinks. Mary felt she had stepped into a dark underworld, and her body shivered. They found a booth and sat down. Immediately, a waitress appeared to take their order. As they sat with their drinks, a man sat down without being invited. He was about forty years old with a dirty, sweaty black beard. He wore a crisp white shirt, red tie, and a gold tie pin with a large diamond in the centre. He also wore gold cufflinks and an Armani three-piece suit with a huge Rolex watch on his arm. His hands were dressed in large gold rings on each finger. He looked like a Don. Mary shuddered when he looked at her with his steely gaze as he gave her a sleazy smile, showing three bright gold teeth. Then he turned to Brian and spoke,

"So, this little beauty is to replace Marisol. What happened to her?"

Then, while glancing at Mary, he asked;

"What can she do to please me?"

Brian was respectful and yielding as he answered the Don, but Mary could sense that he was afraid of him. That pleased her, knowing that someone scared him, which made her respect the Don even more.

Brian answered,

"Marysol decided that she didn't want to be part of our team anymore."

The Don pondered Brian's answer while nodding his head. Then he said again,

"But what can SHE do to please me?"

Brian replied,

"Put some music on and let her behind the bar, then you will see for yourself."

The Don liked his challenge as he smiled and put his fist under his greasy chin to contemplate it. After a bit of thought, he nodded his head in agreement and answered in a warning voice while smiling,

"OK, amigo, let us see what she can do."

There was a tense few seconds as they waited for Mary to get up, Brian and Skips' eyes were glued to her as they waited for her to move. Suddenly, the Don stood up, clapping his hands three times. The music stopped, and there was a silence in the lounge. The Don announced in Spanish that they had a gringo who was going to put on a little show for them. He said to clear the bar and give her a little space. Mary knew every word he had spoken, but didn't let on. She also knew that this display should be the best she ever put on, as if her life depended on it. She looked at Brian with hatred in her eyes for putting her in such a dangerous situation. Brian looked back at Mary worriedly with a pleading look on his face as beads of sweat rolled down from his forehead. Mary knew there was no backing out now. When the disco music started, she stood up, smiling and flamboyantly threw her hands in the air. She had seen many a drag queen doing the same thing back in Tenerife, and at this very second, she missed them all terribly. She also thought of her aunt Sheila, who taught her everything she knew and hoped she would do her proud. She also knew she had to make this one of the best shows she had ever put on.

As the people clapped, Mary sashayed behind the bar, wriggling and clapping to get the crowd going. Then she got into her rhythm and started juggling and flicking bottles, while placing them in front of her along the bar. When she was happy with what ingredients she wanted, she juggled six shot glasses at a time until she had the whole bar lined up. Swinging and dancing, she filled every glass for people to sample. Then she juggled cocktail glasses into position, this time being more careful not to drop a glass because that would ruin the show. She knew this from when she was a child and had the odd mishap. Shot glasses were easy, but large cocktail glasses were more awkward to juggle and would shatter loudly if dropped. Mary continued mesmerising her audience to the disco beat as she danced around, mixing beautiful cocktails especially for the Don and his entourage. When they were ready, she took one off the bar and danced her way over to his table, placing her creation in front of him to sample. As she waited, he slowly looked up into her eyes, then he looked down at his drink, considering whether he should test it or not. Mary waited with bated breath, hoping he would at least taste the drink because if he didn't, she knew it would cause a big problem for them all. Seconds passed before the Don decided to taste his drink; there was complete silence as he took a sip. After tasting it, he licked his lips before standing up and announcing in Spanish.

" Bueno."

While throwing his hands in the air. He grabbed Mary by the shoulders, pulling her to him and kissing her on both cheeks. Everyone in the lounge clapped and cheered as Mary returned to her booth, totally drained from her ordeal. The look of relief on Brian's face said it all as she sat down. Mary just glared at him, asking when they could go home. Brian answered that they had to complete their business first, then they would leave. As they were leaving, they were stopped at the door by the Don. He singled out Mary and addressed her, saying that he had enjoyed her performance, then he placed five hundred dollars into her hand. While he was holding her hand, he noticed the chain on her wrist. He held it up, looking at the little Panther dangling, and he flicked it with his finger before saying,

"I see you belong to the Panther, but if you ever feel like straying, my door is always open to you. Or, if you ever wanted to perform for me privately, I would make sure you were well rewarded."

His hands were hot and sweaty as he smiled at her. Mary could feel a shiver go down her spine as if she were talking to the devil. She muttered a thank you for the tip and smiled weakly, then left with the others.

19

The next day, Brian's car was delivered back to the motel. And without saying a word, they headed to the border. Again, Mary's heart was pounding in her chest as they edged bit by bit to the crossing in a line of traffic. Mary knew that somewhere in the car, there were drugs hidden, and she dreaded the thought of what would happen to her if they were caught. As they arrived at the customs point, Brian handed over their Irish passports, saying they were enjoying a few days touring around. The customs officer eyed them suspiciously. Mary thought her chest would burst, and she would wet her pants. The officer finally closed their passports and told them to move on, calling out next to the vehicle behind. When they got back to the apartment, Brian dropped off Mary before heading away to deliver his car to a garage to be cleared out.

When Mary closed the door behind her, she let go of her emotions and broke down crying. She knew for sure that Brian and Skip had always been in cahoots as drug mules, and now they had made Mary as bad as they were themselves. But even worse than that, she also knew for sure that Brian had something to do with Marisol's death, which made her an accessory to murder. She sobbed and wondered if her life could go any lower. When Brian got back, he was elated; he was also carrying a bag full of dollars. He immediately put the money into the wall safe with their passports and locked it. He went to Mary, wrapping his big arms around her, saying that they were back in the good times and their only way from now on was up. He also thanked her for her great performance, as the Don loved her and wanted them to repeat their business arrangements. Mary was indignant; she told Brian that this was the first and last time she would ever be involved in their drug pushing.

And what's more, she was finishing with Brian and returning to Ireland as soon as she could arrange a flight home. Once again, Brian exploded, and he punched Mary in the solar plexus, winding her. He dragged her across the floor by the hair to the couch, propping her up on the seat. When he had her full attention, he looked into her eyes menacingly, saying,

"Do you think you can just walk away that easily from a winning team that I have just created? A team that I have killed for, just for you. And now that we have reached the crest of the wave, you want to abandon ship? Listen to me, girl, you are going nowhere. Your place is here by my side, we are a winning couple, and no one can touch us now. Not the college, or that old man who thinks he's your grandfather. There is only one way to separate this team, and that is if one of us is dead. And I have no intention of going anywhere, and neither are you."

Over the next two years, things went from bad to worse for Mary. In that time, three more trips were made to Mexico. Mary would perform for the Don; in turn, he would tip her five hundred dollars. Brien would take that money and deposit it in the safe that Mary had no access to because he changed the combination regularly. Her college salary was also deposited into their joint bank account, and she was given a joint debit card, so all her transactions could be monitored by Brian. Of course, Mary never needed for anything; she could buy the most expensive bags, jewellery, or clothes she wished. But everything was monitored, including Mary; she knew she was constantly being followed. If not by

Brian, it would be one of his goons, or even a student when she was at work. Her only hope of privacy was when she went swimming or jogging. She also knew now that the gold bracelet she wore had a tracking device hidden somehow inside the Panther trinket. She found this out by accident because one day she forgot to put it on after swimming and left it at home. Brian was waiting for her return. The first thing that would happen was a punch to the solar plexus, winding her. Then he would urinate on her, letting her know that she was his bitch and he was marking his territory. Lovemaking ceased to exist between them as he had two or three other girls on the go. But whenever he felt in the mood, he would wait until she was showering and slip in behind her. It was never the same as the first time because to Mary, it felt like he was raping her. She always felt violated afterwards; there was no love or affection in his black heart. Mary did try to escape a couple of times. She had found the safe combination under a drawer, and when she opened it to steal her passport to get away, a silent alarm went off, informing Brian. Mary paid dearly for that mistake. Another time, she spirited Ed away from his computations. She told him she was in serious trouble and needed to get out of the country. She needed cash to make a break for Canada, so she gave Ed some of her jewellery to sell. Ed could see she was desperate and told her he would do everything to help her, but to be very careful of Brian because he had become a very dangerous man. Mary waited and prayed that Ed would bring her cash soon, but he never appeared. A few days later, word came back that Ed's car was blindsided while stopped at a red light. The driver of the other car just got out and ran away. It was discovered afterwards that that car was stolen. That evening, Mary noticed that as Brian came out of the shower, he had a red welt across his shoulder. When she inquired what had happened to him, he grunted something about a football tackle and went quickly into the other room to get dressed. Mary had her suspicions about who was driving the stolen car. She went to see Ed in the hospital and was shocked and heartbroken to see him on a ventilator. His leg was also raised in plaster, and he had cuts and bruises all over his body. Mary knew then that even to try and get help would cause people severe pain or even death, so she stopped trying. When she got back from visiting Ed, all the items she had given him to sell were back in her jewellery box. Mary cried alone in her room, knowing she had caused Ed's suffering. Whenever Rose would ring, Mary found it very difficult to talk to her. She thought to herself, how could she ever explain the awful situation she was in? Mary was also terrified that her mother might suggest she visit her for fear of what Brian would do. Mary was in no doubt of what he was capable of. On another occasion, Rose indicated that she intended to visit with Sheila for a week or so. Mary was petrified. She came up with a story that she and Brian were planning a trip to the Rockies. Another time, she told her mother that she had already booked a holiday home to Ireland, around the same time Joe wanted to visit her. Mary hated the lies, but it was the only way she had of keeping her loving family safe. With Brian's association with the cartels, she knew how easily they could arrange a fatal car crash. She would give her own life first rather than let anything happen to them.

20

One morning, as Mary got out of bed, she felt her stomach churn and ran for the toilet to vomit. This happened a couple of times, and Mary didn't understand what was wrong. As she lay on the bed, it dawned on her that she hadn't had her period the previous month. The realisation and horror of being pregnant nearly drove her over the edge of reason. She remembered hearing about gangs that got women pregnant. Then, took their child away to hold them captive so they would do their bidding. Mary knew that Brian would be very capable of doing something like that to her. Mary knew then that her situation was even more desperate than she had imagined. If she didn't get away, she would be shackled to Brian for the rest of her life. While she lay there trying to find a way to get away from him, she had an epiphany as an escape plan came together. She also knew how dangerous it would be, because if she failed, this time, Brian would surely kill her and her baby. She put her plan together, and although at that moment he didn't know it, the Don would play a big part in her escape. But Mary would have to wait for the next drug run to activate it. In preparation, Mary had to be seen by Brian jogging twice a day, morning and evening, no matter what the weather was like. When he commented on this, Mary said that she was going into training to run a marathon. Brien didn't seem to care what she did, so Mary put the first part of her plan into action. As she trained hard, she waited and got fitter for the run of her life. Finally, the time arrived for the drug run. Mary knew that this was the only time the Irish passports would appear as they were necessary to cross the border. When they got home from the drug run, their passports would disappear again into the safe.

Skip didn't need to travel with them anymore as he had already set up the deal with the Don. It also looked better for Brian and Mary to travel as a young, loving couple on a weekend away. Their journey down and crossing the border went as normal. When they got to the motel, as usual, they were frisked by the guards before going upstairs to their room. As they were unpacking, Mary took out her tracksuit and runners to go jogging. When Brian saw this, he asked her what was going on. Mary explained that she had been sitting all day in the car and wanted to stretch her legs. She continued that the marathon was getting close, and she wanted to keep up her training. Brian looked dubious, but Mary explained that there was a small park across the road, which could be seen from the motel where she could train. Brian opened the door and looked across at the park. He could see that it was clearly visible from the motel, so he agreed to let Mary go jogging.

Before she went, he checked that she was wearing her bracelet. Then he told the guard on the top floor to keep an eye on her. The guard knew only too well what Brian meant because, in Mexico, people were kidnapped very easily. Especially people in the drug trade with other cartels for bargaining purposes. So, as Mary ran, he kept his eyes always peeled on her. Mary spent about an hour running around the track, then returned to the motel, sweating and smiling happily at the guard as she passed him. Before she went into her room, she started her stretching exercise. She held on to the banister while putting her leg over it, giving him a nice view. Then she bent over seductively while the guard glanced at her from time to time, enjoying the show. When Mary felt he had seen enough, she sighed loudly and went inside the room, closing the door behind her.

The next part of her plan came when they reached the nightclub. As usual, they were shown to their booth. Once they were settled, and as regulars, drinks were brought to the table free of charge. Brian was his usual flamboyant self, tipping and winking at the waitresses, trying to pick one to be with later that night. Mary knew that this was the norm, and Brian wouldn't go back with her to the motel. He would spend the whole night at the nightclub, then come back early the next morning like a tomcat. Mary looked around; she felt everything she had planned had worked so far. She waited for the Don to appear for their business deal to take place and hoped he would be on time. Because Mary knew that timing was essential in her escape plan. When the Don arrived, Mary made it her business to catch his attention, something she never did before. The Don was intrigued by her behaviour and came over. Mary asked him if he would like to see her performance now? Mary said that she had concocted a special new cocktail in his honour. She told him that she had named the new cocktail ... THE DON, and she wanted to see if he liked it before he had anything else to drink. What she really wanted to do was get her performance over as quickly as possible to keep her plan in motion. The Don was intrigued as to what this new cocktail was, and he agreed eagerly to Mary's request. As before, the Don called for silence, and the disco music started playing. Immediately, Mary jumped up and began performing one of the best shows she had ever put on. When she was finished, she placed her new cocktail before the Don to taste, smiling in anticipation. When he tasted his drink, he stood up and shouted,

"Magnifico."

Everyone clapped to Mary's delight as she turned and bowed to her audience. When Mary went back to her seat, Brian was looking at her with an impressive smile, knowing that she had endeared herself to the Don. He knew that this would be good for his business and gave her an encouraging wink. He told her that she had put on a great show tonight and congratulated her. Mary knew he genuinely meant what he said and was happy to see him smiling. While she had him in such a good mood, Mary asked,

"Do you mind if I go back to the motel early, as I feel a little tired from my training session today?"

She continued,

"I didn't think the heat would be so oppressive down here when I was running around the track."

Brian thought for a second, then, smiling back at her, he waved his hand saying,

" You go on back to the motel and have a good rest, and we will catch up in the morning."

Mary already knew he had arranged for himself another partner for the night. The limousine to escort her back to the hotel was waiting outside. As she was leaving, she approached the Don to say goodnight. Surprised she was leaving so early, but also enjoying his cocktail, he thanked her again. Then he tipped her the usual five hundred dollars. Mary thanked him and put it in her clutch bag. It was still early when she got back to the motel and still bright, but a little dusky. As soon as Mary closed the door to her room, she searched high and low until she found her passport, knowing that Brian wouldn't have carried it out at night. Brian's passport was also there, so she took that as well. As the clock was ticking, she immediately changed out of her dress and put on her body-hugging tracksuit, runners, and a baseball cap.

Stepping out onto the balcony, the guard was surprised to see her and asked what was happening. Mary started stretching, and while she did so, she told him that she wanted to get a few quick laps in before bedtime. The guard was confused whether to let her go or not. But Mary assured him that she was only going over to the park and would be back before it got dark. The guard nervously agreed and placed himself on the balcony so he could always see her. He didn't notice that Mary had her five hundred dollars and two passports strategically placed around her body-hugging tracksuit so he wouldn't notice. When he stepped back to let her pass, she smiled at him, then bounded down the steps to the car park. She made another show of stretching and bending over for the next guard before jogging across the car park heading for the park. As she crossed the busy road leading to the park gate, she tore off the bracelet on her arm, clasping the Panther in her hand.

As an open-backed truck passed her, she threw the Panther into the back, then carried on jogging. Once she was in the park, she very slowly jogged a couple of laps so the guard could see her. She knew that at the other side of the park, there was a small break in the fence where she could easily slip through. Also, there were a couple of wheelie bins blocking the view of the guard. As the guard relaxed a little, watching Mary slowly jogging in circles, he looked down at his phone to check his emails. When he looked up, Mary was gone.

21

Immediately, a rescue operation was mounted by the cartel as darkness fell. The guards were punched and kicked for letting Mary go into the park in the first place. Secondly, all available hoods were notified to look out for Mary. Her description was sent out far and wide across Tijuana. Brian activated his tracking device on the Panther, and all local taxi stands were checked to see if she was picked up. When they eventually caught up with the open-backed truck, the poor, unfortunate farmer who hadn't had a clue of what was going on was tortured to within an inch of his life to divulge her whereabouts. By first light, all trace of Mary was lost.

A dishevelled Brian stood on the balcony of the motel looking across at the park, not really believing Mary could have been kidnapped. She was only small fry in the grand scheme of things and wouldn't amount to much if she were needed as a bargaining chip for the cartel. He decided to walk across the road to investigate. As he got to the kerb at the far side of the road, something shiny caught his eye. There, lying against the path in the gutter, was a broken gold bracelet. Brian picked it up and continued into the park. As he walked around slowly, checking where Mary would have jogged, he followed her path. He got around to the hole in the fence where a wheelie bin was blocking the view of the guard's vantage point. Then, as the realisation hit him, he ran back across the road through beeping and breaking traffic until he reached the motel room. Immediately, he checked his holdall, where both their passports were hidden. When he saw they were gone, and he knew that Mary had taken them, he slowly rose from his knees. In temper, he closed his fist tightly around the broken bracelet until his hand bled. Immediately, word was sent to all border crossings out of Tijuana. But nothing was found of a single girl wearing a tracksuit and a baseball cap.

22

Mary sat shivering in fear behind a locked door of the ladies' toilet in Cancun airport, she was waiting for her connecting flight to Chicago O'Hare airport. So far, her plan had worked, but until she was sitting in her seat flying out of Mexico to Chicago, she didn't feel safe. When she had started her run, she remembered slipping through the hole in the fence after slowly jogging around the park so the guards would relax. Then, on her fourth lap, the clock started ticking. As soon as she got through the hole in the fence, she sprinted like a bat out of hell through the streets of Tijuana. She passed many taxi stands until she felt she was far enough away to hail a cab, tipping the driver extra to speed faster to Tijuana International Airport. On arrival, she rushed in to book the first red-eye flight anywhere out of Tijuana, which turned out to be Cancun. She knew in advance that it was her only option. She also knew there was an early flight from Cancun to Chicago and planned to purchase a ticket to Dublin from there. But, at this point, while in Mexico, she knew she was still in great danger if recognised as she waited for her flight to board. When the time came, she pulled her cap down over her eyes as she walked quickly through the terminal towards American immigration. Her heart pounded, and she knew cartel goons had eyes everywhere. To be caught now at this last stage of her escape would mean the end of her life and her unborn child. As she reached pre-boarding inspection, Mary removed her cap, pushing her hair back and smiling at the immigration officer who checked her passport. When he asked the purpose of her visit, she repeated the exact words as Brian always did,

"I'm just returning after a few days touring around."

He asked if she was carrying anything. Mary answered that, unfortunately, her case had been stolen, and she had nothing to declare. As she was obviously not carrying any goods or luggage, the officer stamped her passport and waved her on. Mary walked through into the safe area for boarding; her relief was so great that she started to cry. A concerned passenger stopped to see if she was

OK. Mary just smiled and said she was fine. She told the passenger that she had just broken up with her boyfriend and was a little sad. Placated, the passenger smiled back and said,

"There were plenty more fish in the sea, and a girl as pretty as she could do a lot of fishing."

Mary smiled back, saying,

"Thank you, but I won't be fishing for a very long time, or maybe never again."

On landing in O'Hare airport, a more relaxed Mary checked all flights for Dublin, hoping she could afford one as the last of her cash was running low. Her luck was holding as she secured a homeward flight with a few dollars left over that she changed into euros before boarding. She didn't purchase anything in O'Hare as she knew she would get something to eat on the plane and needed to preserve the last of her money. Even at this stage, she couldn't eat anything because of her condition, but she was happy; she had escaped.

23

Eight months later, Mary lay on her back, moaning, puffing, breathing, blowing. Her contractions were coming regularly as Rose sat beside her, encouragingly telling her to push. A red-faced Mary, now nearly exhausted, was swearing. She was promising her mother that she would never have sex again. And she also swore that when the baby was born, she was not keeping it. When it was all over, they placed the little bundle on her chest. Mary cried with love to see her beautiful daughter with a wisp of red hair. Afterwards, Mary went into a deep, deep sleep. When she was down in the depths of slumber, she dreamt. Sitting at the edge of the bed was her grandmother holding her baby in her arms. She smiled proudly at Mary as she gently rocked her baby as it slept, and Mary was happy.

Mary did try to reconnect with her friend June. Her father had opened a new car showroom in Galway, and June was their executive salesperson. When Mary phoned, June was genuinely delighted to receive her call. She asked excitedly about her mam and dad, and if they were in good health. She also asked if she was happy to be home in Ireland again, skilfully avoiding the question about Brian. Mary could feel the tension between them, so she decided to tell June that they had split up and Brian had stayed in the USA. They talked happily about Mary living in Stoneybatter with her daughter, Rosemary. June told her about her travels to Cambodia and Vietnam, then eventually visiting Australia.

Mary felt a little envious knowing that she had missed her opportunity to travel as a young carefree girl. Instead, she let herself be groomed and manipulated by Brian into drug pushing. As their conversation was coming to an end, and to allay Mary's fears, June told her that she never told anyone about Brian or his drug dealing. She also said that she was very happy she was finished with him for good. The call ended cordially with the two friends promising that they would meet for coffee sometime. But as Mary hung up, she knew in her heart and soul that they wouldn't. Sadly, she knew that their friendship had run its course. She couldn't blame June for not wanting to keep in touch, as their lives had gone in two completely different directions. Mary remembered how badly she had behaved the day they parted in LAX when June tried everything to get her on that flight home to Dublin. As she put her phone back in her bag, Mary's stomach churned, knowing how stupid she had been for not listening to her best friend. But now it was too late.

For the next four years, they settled into quiet normality. The feeling that Mary had previously of being watched or followed disappeared completely. Mary stood with all the other parents, seeing their children graduating from creche. She thought her heart would burst with love and pride to see her little daughter. She was dressed in her long red gown with a mortarboard on top of her beautiful Auburn hair that matched her outfit. When they had finished their little party piece and sang, everyone clapped and awed as the children ran to their parents. Rosemary, who was named after both her grandmother and great-grandmother, ran to be cuddled and kissed by Mary, Rose, and Frank on her special day,

"Next year I will be five years old and starting in big school at Stanhope St, Rosemary proudly exclaimed."

Mary was so happy with this because they lived close by in Oxmanstown Road, Stoneybatter, in North Dublin's Inner City. Her mother Rose and auntie Sheila had grown up in that small two-up, two-down, red and yellow-bricked terraced house. They were also embraced by the local community, who remembered her grandparents fondly. It was just perfect for them both, where she felt at home and safe. Mary loved living so close to Dublin city centre, it had every amenity a city had to offer, as well as living in a close-knit, friendly community. She was also a third-year student studying law at the local law library. Life was kind to The Honeys, as they liked to call themselves. They had turned their little girly house into a pink haven. Whenever Mary needed a babysitter, Rose and Frank were only too happy to step in. Or when she visited Tenerife, she had an entourage of people fighting to mind Rosemary and take her out for treats. So, Mary was looking forward to their summer holidays with her whole family. She enjoyed the sunshine and madness of the Queen Vick drag bar and restaurant.

A few days before they were due to fly out, The Honeys went shopping to get presents for Sheila, Conchita, and Joe. It was Rosemary's idea because when they came to visit, they would always bring her presents. They were having a lovely day out in town, just walking around window shopping, until they stopped at a travel agent. Mary glanced at the special offers in the window; one offer in particular caught her eye. She shuddered as she read the special offer. It felt like someone had walked over her grave. The offer read, "five-star holiday for a three-star price with flights to LAX." Mary pulled Rosemary's hand to get away from the window as fast as she could. For the rest of the day, she felt on edge; whenever she passed a window or mirror, she checked behind herself that she wasn't being followed or watched. Just then, her phone rang, and when she answered, it was Rose sounding concerned at the other end. She asked Mary if she was OK. Mary replied yes, but inquired as to why she had rung her? Rose said that she had a premonition and needed to know she was OK. Mary knew what Rose was trying to say and told her she was fine. She continued their conversation, saying she was in town getting the last few bits and pieces for their holidays. The call ended between mother and daughter, but when they hung up, there was still a feeling of impending doom. Before they left for home, at one stage, Mary thought she saw a shadow move. When she looked behind her, nobody was there. Mary chastised herself, thinking she was getting paranoid, but still felt something was amiss. That night, while Mary fitfully slept, she dreamed that she was running through a fog. As she ran, her legs were getting heavier. It was getting harder to lift her legs, then the mist lifted, and she could see Rosemary running ahead of her. She tried to catch up, but the more she tried, the harder it got to lift her legs. It felt like lead weights were attached to them. Rosemary was getting further away from her. Mary called out for her to wait. Rosemary kept on running. In panic, Mary cried out again and again until her grandmother appeared. She was tapping her on the arm, encouraging her to run faster after her daughter. But she couldn't reach her; her grandmother tapped her even more. Then Mary woke up from her dream to see Rosemary tapping her on the arm. Rosemary stood beside her bed, half asleep and rubbing her eyes. She said that she heard her mother calling her. Mary's heart stopped racing, and her breathing settled as the realisation of waking her daughter dawned on her. She spoke softly to Rosemary, saying,

"It's OK, baby, I'm sorry I woke you; mammy was having a bad dream, that's all."

Then she pulled back her bed covers for Rosemary to get in beside her. While cuddling her daughter, Mary thought to herself, I will be glad to get away on this holiday. Then she closed her eyes and tried to go back to sleep.

24

Mary was glad when the day arrived for their flight to Tenerife, although, even in the airport, she still checked behind herself. It was great to be back. Mary loved the heat, the sea, the palm trees, and, of course, the bougainvillaea cascading over walls and fences. At night, she would do the odd shift behind the bar and join in the fun of the drag shows. Within a couple of days, she was totally relaxed again. One sunny afternoon, while catching a few rays on the beach as Rosemary was building sandcastles, Mary dozed off for a few moments. When she opened her eyes again, Rosemary was gone. She jumped up panic stricken, just then, her phone rang. When she answered the call, still casting her eyes around to find her daughter. Mary froze as Rosemary spoke, saying,

"Hi mammy, Brian and I are having ice cream in McDonald's, and Brian wants to know if you would like to come up and join us?"

McDonald's was situated just behind where Mary had been lying out. She turned around to see Rosemary and Brian waving from the promenade. As Mary made her way across the sand to the promenade, the pain in her gut was so intense, she started to whimper in fear. When she reached McDonald's, Rosemary called out, saying excitedly,

"Look, mommy, Brian bought me a big 99," as she relished the ice cream.

Brian spoke first with a smirk on his face, saying,

"Well, isn't this a nice, happy family gathering, and you never told me we had a daughter."

Petrified and begging, all Mary could say was,

"Don't hurt her, please."

Brian, giving her the look of innocence, said,

"Why would I hurt my own flesh and blood?"

Mary just hung her head, afraid to speak. Then Brian's eyes hardened, and he asked the question,

"Have you still got it?"

Mary didn't lift her head because she knew exactly what he meant. Mary always carried his passport with her. She felt safe when it was in her possession because she knew if she had it, Brian couldn't follow her to Europe. Obviously, she had been mistaken. Mary nodded yes, still not lifting her head. At this answer, Brian gave her a broad, triumphant smile, saying,

"Well, do you think I should have it back?"

Totally defeated and petrified, Mary nodded yes. Then she told him that she didn't have it at the beach but would get it for him. Brian thought for a moment while Mary held her breath. To Mary's relief, Brian agreed, saying she could bring it to him, and he would let her know where and when. Mary agreed immediately. Brian looked at Mary with that evil look she had become accustomed to in America. He warned her by saying,

"You saw how easy it is to find you, and as a family man, I would be very sad to have to make necessary choices. Do you understand what I mean?"

Mary knew only too well what Brian's warning meant. So again, she agreed immediately and submissively. As soon as Brian was gone, Mary grabbed Rosemary, who was enjoying her ice cream and hugged her tightly, then she collected her things off the beach and made a run for the Queen Vick. Joe was cleaning up around the front of the pub and saw her running towards him. He knew instantly from the look on her face that something was terribly wrong. He ran to her, asking what had happened while lifting Rosemary into his arms. Mary was distraught and shaking; all she wanted to do was get inside the pub and lock the doors. When she told Joe what had happened, he got on the phone, and a family meeting was arranged immediately. When everyone was assembled, and the dangerous situation Mary and Rosemary found themselves in was explained to everyone, a plan had to be put together for their safety first and foremost. The family listed out the possibilities of what Brian wanted.

1. Could Rosemary be spirited away to a safe house?

2   Could Brian be bought off?

3. How could the finances be raised?

4. What limit, if any, could they go to?

5.   Would it be wise to involve the police?

As the conversation continued, Mary stood up to make a statement. When everyone went quiet, she spoke, saying,

"I know you all mean well, and I am so grateful to you all for your wonderful support. But it is I who got myself into this awful situation. I think the best thing I can do now is meet with Brian to see what he wants. Maybe I can reason with him to leave us alone. Until we know what he wants, it would mean I would have to keep running for the rest of my life. If somehow, we can agree to something, like a bribe, and his passport back. Which I intend to give him as soon as he makes contact. After that, we will have to wait and see."

There was a lot of misgiving around the room, with most of them agreeing with Mary. It was also decided that Rosemary would be taken to Conchita and Sheila's apartment, because it was the most secure. Rose would also stay with her until the situation was resolved.

25

It was a further two days before Brian made contact. He told Mary that he was disappointed not to be able to see his child out and about getting fresh air and playing. Sneeringly, he said it is what all children need to help them grow. Mary was ready for his call and had prepared herself mentally. She wasn't going to be intimidated like before, once Rosemary was safe. She knew she could be strong enough to cope with whatever happened next, even if Brian killed her. She knew if she were murdered, her grandmother would be waiting for her with open arms. When Brian felt her defiance on the phone, he got to the point of the call. He wanted her to come to the house he had rented, but gave no address. He told her to come alone and not bring any mobile phone or tracking device. He gave her instructions to get the 467 bus to San Juan village from Adeje. She was to get off at the last stop at the end of the town. She was to wait for him there, and he would meet her when he was ready. He also warned her to bring his passport and wear a lovely dress for dinner. Then he threatened her again not to cross him or there would be severe consequences. Mary shuddered when he hung up because the thought of meeting him again made her skin crawl. Having to dine with him meant he wanted more than dinner. She was prepared to do anything to appease him if she could convince him to leave them alone. She would accept any indignity he suggested, including paying him an enormous ransom afterwards. When the day arrived, and not knowing if she would live or die, Mary went to see Rosemary. She played with her all day. When the time came to go, she hugged and kissed her daughter, knowing it could be the very last time she would hold her. Mary's heart was breaking as she walked to catch the bus alone. When she reached the appointed stop, she got off the bus and waited. There were other passengers at the stop waiting for another bus. When the bus came, they all boarded, and Mary was left alone. She knew the area she was in and was familiar with the roads around her. But when Brian appeared out of nowhere, she got a fright. He just smiled at her, saying,

"Let's go for a walk, follow me."

As they walked together, nothing was said, then just outside the village, Brian turned up a side road leading to a private finca. As Mary approached the small house, she could understand why Brian rented this one. There were no security cameras to record his coming and going. She was very surprised when he opened the front door to see an ultra-modern interior. The ceilings went right up into the eaves with modern lighting and chandeliers. All the walls were painted white with beautiful, coloured paintings hung around the sides. The cream floor tiles throughout the house were bright and highly polished. There were colourful rugs scattered around expensive soft furnishings in the lounge area. Also, the open layout of the area led to a beautiful, fully fitted designer kitchen with black marble counters.

When Mary looked at the dining table, she could see it was set for two with candles and wine glasses. If she weren't there for the reason she was, she would have been very impressed. When she turned to face Brian, his eyes were soft, and his smile was gentle. He asked softly if she would like red or white with the meal. Mary thanked him, suggesting white. Brian went to the fridge while Mary took her seat. Brian placed before her a lovely colourful Mediterranean salad with a basket of fresh breadsticks. He poured the wine and sat down. When they had finished, Mary said that the meal was very nice. Brian smiled back, saying he bought all the ingredients fresh today. Mary nodded her approval. Smiling back and leaving the dishes, Brian suggested they retire to the lounge for drinks. Mary didn't want to drink anymore, because she wanted to keep a clear head for whatever came next. But Brian insisted on pouring her another glass while opening a bottle of beer for himself. When they sat down on the soft couch, Brian asked Mary if she had brought it? Knowing he wanted to get straight to business first, without batting an eyelid, Mary opened her clutch bag and handed him his passport, saying nothing. Carrying on in a normal voice, he said,

"I'm relieved to have this back as I have been travelling on forged documents supplied by the cartel for the last four years."

Brian got up and went into the bedroom to put the passport away. When he returned, Mary noticed he had changed out of his long trousers into a loose

T-shirt, shorts, and was barefoot. Looking totally relaxed, he sat back down again. As he sat back on the couch, he exclaimed that he was more comfortable now. Mary didn't know whether he was talking about the fact that he was wearing casual gear and barefoot, or that she had given him his passport back. She lifted an eyebrow in question. Brian didn't seem to like that; instantly, his mood changed. Trying to change the subject and keep the conversation convivial. Mary asked casually how Ed was doing after his accident. In all the time after her escape, Ed never left her thoughts. She always felt guilty for involving him in her plan; she hoped he had made a full recovery from his ordeal.

On hearing his name, Brian got angrier. He stared at Mary, choosing his words carefully,

"That meddling old man died before he ever regained consciousness, and it served him right."

Mary wanted to scratch his eyes out as the blood boiled in her body, but somehow, she held her composure and let the subject drop.

Brien continued,

"You left me in a terrible situation back in Mexico. It cost me an awful lot of money, and my standing with the cartel."

Mary answered,

"I'm sorry, Brian, but I was pregnant and afraid of being arrested. I didn't know what to do for the best, and for our child. I felt it was time to go home for everyone's sake."

Brian pondered her answer before saying,

"I would have provided for you both; you would have wanted for nothing."

Mary knew exactly how he would have provided for them by dealing with his shady underworld connections. She knew she didn't want her baby to be dragged down to his level. But Mary didn't want to antagonise him either, so she kept her mouth shut. Then Brian continued,

"We were a great team, and could be again. I missed you when you left me."

Mary answered,

"I've been on my own for four years now, and I like it that way. I am very happy in my life, with my daughter."

Then Brian asked,

"Do you think Rosemary would need a father as well? I never got the opportunity to say what I wanted in our relationship. Do you think I should have been asked if I wanted to be with my child or not?"

Then anger came into his raised voice,

"But for you to run away without even letting me know you were pregnant, then, hide the fact that I had a child of my own. Do you think you were being fair?"

Mary, trying to keep things calm, nodded yes as she noticed Brian was sweating. He was swilling back bottle after bottle of beer as they talked together. She also noticed he was getting tipsy. But before he got much too much to drink, she wanted to find out what it would take for him to go away and leave them alone. She knew she would have to address the elephant in the room. Mary asked the question,

"Brian, you have your passport back now, so does that mean you are going to go back to the USA?"

Brian, laughing out loud, said,

"No, sweetheart, not now, not now that I have found out I have a daughter. And I also have you back again. You and I are a great team; we have made our own little girl together. We could also make a great life together, here in Tenerife. It would be great; you already work in a successful pub business, and I have contacts in Morocco. You and Rosemary could mesmerise the crowd mixing cocktails, and I could expand our business interests with the cartels. Together we would be unstoppable, and the most successful family on the island."

Mary couldn't believe her ears. She now understood that, not his passport, or even giving him money, would get him out of their lives. She also knew that he had built up this fantasy in his head. He was planning to drag Rosemary and herself down into the underworld with him, using Rosemary as an asset. She started to panic and wanted to get away from Brian as fast as she could. She stood up quickly and said she wanted to leave;

she repeated, she wanted to leave, now. Brian stood up, holding her by the shoulders, looking confused because, in his twisted mind, he thought the evening was going great, and they were getting back together as a family. Mary kept saying, I want to leave, I want to leave now, while raising her voice. Brian started to lose his temper, pushing her back down on the couch while throwing himself on top of her, pinning her down. Mary stopped wriggling and knew what was going to happen next. She knew if she let him have his way, she might be able to get away afterwards. She let him kiss her; she could feel his mouth on hers, then his tongue searching and exploring as he used to do. His lips moved down along her neck, kissing and nuzzling gently. Suddenly, and roughly, he grabbed her by the waist. He flipped her over, forcing her face and head down while raising her hips. Mary knew exactly what was coming next; he had done this so many times before. But this time, she was not letting it happen. With a newfound strength, she pushed back with all her power. She knocked Brian off balance, and they both fell off the couch to the floor. Quickly, Mary jumped up and made to run for the door. Just as she was about to open the door, Brian threw himself against it. Sweating and panting, he told her she was going nowhere as he was not finished with her yet.

Mary could see the same viciousness in his eyes that he used to have before when he was raping her. She darted to the kitchen, making for the knife block to defend herself. But like the Panther he was, Brian grabbed her arm, knocking the knife from her hand, pinning her against the marble counter, hurting her back. He spun her around again, pushing her head forward while lifting her skirt and pulling at her pants. But Mary fought back, screaming at him and elbowing him in the jaw. It knocked him back so she could turn around to face him again. Then came the crippling blow, into the solar plexus. Mary could feel the excruciating pain as the wind was knocked out of her, and she fell to the ground, coughing and gasping for air. As she lay there writhing on the ground, she looked up at Brian, who was in a mad temper. His face was contorted with rage. She watched him take out his penis and start to urinate over her. She knew when he was finished, he would drag her to the shower and rape her. But the fight was not gone out of her yet. She screamed up at him that he was only a filthy animal, and he would never get near her or her daughter, ever. Because she was not subdued and whimpering on the floor, it made Brian angrier. In his fury, he lifted his leg to stamp on Mary's head. Mary could see it coming and covered herself, expecting the blow. It never came; somehow, when Brian lifted his right leg, and because the floor was wet from his urine, his left leg shot out from under him. He lifted into the air and came down heavily. His head hit the marble counter with a sickening crack as he fell lifeless to the floor.

26

There was total silence as Mary slowly got to her knees to see Brian lying motionless on the floor. Blood was seeping from his ear and nose. By the time she stood up, it was beginning to form into a pool. Mary knew she had to get help, but she had no phone, she ran to Brian's bedroom to see if she could find his. She rummaged through the bedroom until she found his mobile phone, but she didn't know his passcode. She knew if she put the wrong passcode in three times, it would be locked out, and then it would go to emergency calls only. When this happened, with shaking hands, Mary started to dial 112, the emergency number. As she dialled, 1 ... 1 ... she stopped. As she got to the last digit, Mary lifted her head to think for a moment, then pressed cancel. Slowly, she walked back into the kitchen, where Brian lay motionless in the same position. Ever so quietly, Mary knelt beside him and stared into his face. Suddenly, Brian opened his eyes, on seeing Mary, he whispered the words,

"Please, help me."

Mary whispered in his ear,

"Help you ... help you do what ... destroy my life, Rosemary's life, and my family's life and business. I don't think so, Brian, do you?"

Mary continued,

"Look what you have done with your own life, and the opportunities you've had. You could have travelled anywhere in the world, and the fabulous life and places you could have had and seen. Or think about the good you could have done as a football player, then eventually, coach and mentor, respected and revered, just like Ed. And now, you have wasted all your talent, for the sake of money and drug pushing that leads to misery and death for anyone with whom you come into contact. But Brian, you should know this now, that your biggest loss was my love for you. Yes, Brian, it was you, it was always you. I would have gone to hell and back for your love to be returned to me. The wonderful, loving man I met on that flight to LAX over nine years ago. As you lie here like the devil you have become, with nothing but hatred in your murderous black heart, I feel no pity or compassion."

Then she finished speaking by saying,

"Don't hang around too long, Marisol and Ed are waiting to greet you."

Mary noticed that his mouth was drooping, and his lips were turning blue. She never touched him but kept staring into his face. After a while, as if in a trance, she stood up again and went to the table where they had eaten. Carefully, she took up her own plate, utensils, and wine glass. She brought them to the sink and, after washing each item, she put them back into the individual cupboards and drawers. She stepped carefully around Brian, lying on the floor. She could hear that his breathing was becoming more laboured. She carried on cleaning and wiping any area she thought she might have touched. As she looked around, she thought to herself, a fingerprint, or anything to indicate that she was there, could get her caught. Then she went to the bathroom and had a shower. When she was finished, she carefully wiped every area that she came into contact with. When she was dressed again, she brought out all the items of clothing, putting them in the washing machine. The dish towel and any cloth she used were put in with washing powder and a drop of bleach. While she was doing this, she gingerly stepped around Brian and listened from time to time to check on his breathing; it had got much shallower now. It was in the early hours of the morning when Brian eventually stopped breathing, and Mary watched as his skin slowly turned to porcelain. She never touched him or the pool of blood around him; she just sat quietly waiting for the sun to rise. At six am, Mary stood at the door and panned the house one last time for any sign she might have been there.

When she was happy, she slowly closed it, giving the doorknob a last wipe. With the sun on her face and a great sadness over Brian's loss, she slowly walked back to the village. She mingled amongst the workers getting on the bus for the Adeje bus station. From there, she immediately took another bus to see her daughter. After she kissed and hugged Rosemary for what seemed like hours, she sat at the breakfast table with Rose, Sheila, and Conchita. They all wanted to know if he had agreed to any terms, and if he did, how much they had to pay? For a while, Mary was lost in her thoughts before she spoke; they all waited for her answer. Mary didn't want to implicate them in any way if it was found out that she was at the house. To protect them from any backlash, Mary had to keep them in the dark as to what really happened. She concocted a story on the way to the apartment. When she was ready to speak, she looked up at them all earnestly, saying,

"He is gone, it's all over, we both talked it through, and he has no interest in ever having anything to do with Rosemary. All he wanted was his Irish passport back, which made life easy for him when passing through borders. He said a family would only tie him down. In his words, he said a kid would ruin his reputation, especially when he returned to the USA. He liked his standing as a high-flying bachelor, with no ties. So that was it, and as soon as I gave him his passport, he wanted to leave for Morocco to close a deal on a big drug shipment."

Rose couldn't believe her ears. She asked again,

"And that is what it was all about, all the time, a fucking stolen Irish passport?"

Mary answered,

"Yes, Mom, and he is leaving Tenerife for Morocco today."

Rose clasped her hands to her face, then, throwing them in the air, she wrapped Mary in a big hug, saying,

"Thank God, it's all over now, we can get on with our own fucking lives."

Mary just nodded, holding her mother's hand in hers. Over the next week, Mary listened to the news and scanned every newspaper. She wanted to see if there was a person found dead in suspicious circumstances. Eventually, a small article appeared in a local newspaper about a tourist dying in a tragic accident. It went on to say the cleaner found him when she came to clean the house, and they think it was alcohol related. Police could not ascertain his identity as he had several passports in his possession. The article went on to say that they had contacted Interpol for assistance to see if he was involved in criminality. But could not find any evidence to prove so. Mary was relieved to read that no investigation was issuing. Towards the end of the summer, another article caught her eye, saying that the tourist found dead was an Irishman. The Irish government was providing consular assistance to his family for his repatriation back to Ireland. Mary put down the paper, knowing that it was finally all over.

27

Rosemary would be starting her new school year soon, so she arranged for her return from Tenerife. When she got home, she also started watching RIP.ie. When Mary was safely home in Stoneybatter and was satisfied that Brian's death would never be connected to her or her family, she confessed everything to Rose. Her mother listened in stunned silence. Afterwards, she put her arms around Mary, saying that it was an awful burden for her to carry alone. As she hugged and kissed Mary, she told her that it was all over now and to move forward with her life. But Mary felt it was not finished with her yet. There was still something niggling at her, and she didn't know what. It was later, when she was reading the death notice in RIP.ie she was following since Brian's death. She knew what she had to do. The notice read that a funeral service would be held for the remains of Brian in Saint Declan's church, Ardmore, County Waterford. Mary wondered why the service would be held so far away from his hometown of Donegal, as it was on the northwest coast of Ireland. Ardmore County Waterford was in the southeast. She had already made up her mind to attend the service, knowing that it would bring closure to everything that had happened in the past. She also wanted to say goodbye to the love of her life, knowing she would finally be able to move on in the future, if love ever came her way again. She would never forget Brian's loving touch, his hand in hers, with so much life and love in his eyes when he looked at her. Her heart ached for him, remembering she loved him deep into her soul and bones. It was a memory she would always treasure before the dark days overtook him. She had come to love him in the darkness, as much as the light, that sometimes spilt from him when drugs and the greed for money weren't involved. When Mary explained to Rose her plans and why she needed to see them through. Rose was very supportive and understanding, saying to take as long as she needed to say her goodbyes, then move on with her life.

Having booked an overnight stay in the centre of Ardmore village at the Tower Hotel, Mary set off alone for the Sunny southeast of Ireland, as it was known and advertised by travel companies. True enough, it lived up to its name as Mary drove along the southeast coast in beautiful sunshine. After passing through the town of Dungarvan, County Waterford, she missed the turn for Ardmore and ended up in another lovely coastal town called Youghal, County Cork. Feeling a little flustered and stressed, she doubled back to find the turnoff she had missed. She knew at this stage she would be running late for the service and decided to go straight to the church. When she eventually reached Ardmore, she drove down through the village towards the sea to Saint Declan's church, which was facing out into Ardmore Bay. As she got out of the car, she had to take a moment to look across the breathtaking vista, the sun glistened and shimmered on the waves lapping onto the golden strand. The beauty of the distant cliff tops and boats in the harbour made her heart soar. She thought to herself, a picture postcard wouldn't be able to capture such beauty as she made her way to the lovely country church. On her way through the churchyard, she noticed a lot of emergency vehicles parked outside. Coast Guard, ambulances, Garda cars, and rescue helicopter vehicles. Being late, she quietly slipped into the last pew so as not to be noticed. As her eyes adjusted to the light, she could see down the aisle of the church. On a table covered with a white linen cloth was an urn placed in front of the altar. Mary knew they were Brian's ashes and blessed herself reverently. The local priest carried on saying mass while the congregation answered his prayers, and Mary also prayed. When it came to the homily, the priest asked for solemn prayers for the bereaved family and friends of Brian. Mary hung her head in prayer, and as she did so, a great sadness of loss came over her. She sat down and sobbed quietly into her handkerchief. When the service finally finished, the priest announced to the congregation to stand, saying,

"Let us take Brian in peace to his last resting place, where his ashes will be scattered in the bay by his family."

Children in football strips holding hurly sticks formed outside as a guard of honour. Then everyone stood up and answered Amen, as the chief mourners stepped out into the aisle. Mary, being at the back, couldn't see past the standing crowd as she waited for Brian's ashes to pass. Then, as the procession reached where Mary was standing, she lifted her head to bless herself as they passed. It was then she saw him; she had to take a second look. She thought she was in some horror movie as she watched. She couldn't believe her eyes. Brian was leading the procession, carrying the urn in his hands. Brian turned to look at her as their eyes met, his eyes widened, and Mary passed out.

28

When she came around, her eyes focused on a little old lady with grey hair tied back tightly in a bun. She was wearing a black dress, and around her neck hung a silver cross and chain that shone brightly in the sunlight. The lady spoke first in a soft Donegal accent,

"Welcome back, Mary. You gave us a terrible shock."

On hearing her name being spoken, Mary started to panic and tried to get up. But the sudden movement as she lifted her head made her feel woozy. The lady calmed her, saying,

"I hope you don't mind, but the ambulance crew checked your bag to ascertain if you needed any medication, just in case you were diabetic, etc. They also found your identity and checked your vitals to make sure you were ok. When they were happy that you just fainted, they let us take over."

Mary looked quickly around to see a modern sitting room; she was lying on a couch with a soft cushion under her head. The lady introduced herself as Kate, which was short for Kathleen. She told Mary that she had fainted in the church. As they lived next door, she was brought here so the others could spread Brian's ashes out in the Bay. Speechless, Mary tried to make sense of what she had seen. She tried to put perspective on her mental state, whether she was cracking up or not. As she was thinking, the door opened, and a big man stood before her with a cup of tea in his hand. Kate said that a hot cup of sweet tea would help her, so Mary sat up to drink it.

Kate introduced her husband Sean and smiled warmly at him as he handed Mary the tea. After a few sips, she began to feel a little better and thanked them both for their kindness. They both tut-tutted her thanks, saying it was the least they could do for a person who would attend their son's service. Mary then realised she was speaking to Brian's parents. She told them how sorry she was for their sad loss, and the two of them bowed their heads sadly, thanking her. Then Kate asked how Mary knew their son Brian? Mary had to think quickly. She told them that years ago, she had lived in the USA and had met him there. She said she was a mixologist at the college where Brian played football. But now she lives in Dublin and had heard Brian had passed and thought she should pay her respects. Kate and Sean, being teetotallers, didn't know what a mixologist was. They thought she was some kind of doctor or pharmacist. Being respectful, they nodded their heads in understanding of what Mary had told them. They were very happy that Mary came to the service and thanked her warmly. As Mary was feeling a lot better now, she decided it was time to leave. Both parents wouldn't hear of it; they said she couldn't go until she met Brian's brother Sean-Og (meaning young Sean in Gaelic). They told her he would be back shortly after scattering Brian's ashes in the bay. They also told Mary how happy they were to have his ashes here, as they would always be close to him.

Mary just smiled in agreement, but dreaded meeting Brian's brother, Sean-Og. When he eventually came back, Mary got her second shock to see Brian again standing in the doorway. As Sean-Og crossed the floor in three steps, he shook Mary's hand. Mary was dumbstruck to hear this big man speak with a soft Donegal accent that sounded so much like Brian's. He had his lovely soft brown eyes and shocking red hair. He told her, as he walked down the church aisle, that he had gotten an awful shock to see her faint. He ran to her assistance, and now he was very glad to see she was fine again. As he spoke, he took her hand in his, so soft and gentle. All Mary could do was stare at him in amazement, knowing that he was Brian's identical twin brother, who was never spoken about. He was dressed in a Coast Guard uniform. He told Mary they had just returned from the rib, having laid Brien to rest. Mary said she was very sorry for his loss. Sean bowed his head sadly and thanked her. As it was getting towards evening, Mary said she'd better check into her hotel. On inquiring where she was staying, Sean's eyes brightened, saying that it was where they were holding a small reception for Brian. He continued that some of the team were already there and offered to escort her. Mary left her car and walked the short stroll to the hotel with Sean. As they did so, she smiled as everybody passing them, especially children, greeted them, saying,

"Hi Sean".

Sean answered each child by name, returning the greeting. When he saw Mary smiling, he explained that he was the manager, coach, and trainer in the local GAA Club. He was also a volunteer fireman and coast guard for the Irish rescue service. He told Mary he had lived in this village most of his life, even as a young trainee lifeguard during the summer months. He said that if he weren't performing lifeguard duties, he would be picking carrots. He had lodgings with the Troy family, who treated him as one of their own. He told her that he just fell in love with the village, and as it was a small village, everyone knew everyone. Mary then understood why all the emergency vehicles were parked outside the church earlier. She also knew that the people and the children's guard of honour were not there for Brian, but as a mark of respect for Sean-Og and his parents. Mary said that she thought he had come from Donegal. This seemed to sadden Sean as he answered that they had, but he didn't elaborate. Mary let the question drop. After Mary checked into the hotel, she was invited to join the group for a drink. Later, when everyone had gone, she decided to have something to eat. Sean asked if he could join her, as he didn't get a chance to eat all day. Having watched Sean for a while, and saw how easily he mingled with his friends who enjoyed his friendly banter. Mary had no objection to his amenable company. During the meal, as they got talking, Mary explained again how she knew Brian from college. She never let on about their relationship or the drug running. Sean listened with interest while she spoke, making Mary relaxed as they got to know each other. Mary asked Sean if they were close as brothers? Sean answered sadly,

"No, we were not close."

Sean continued,

"Brian had his own demons, and as his brother, he couldn't advise him. He was a bit of a wild child, making the family unpopular in our village in Donegal. I also had a problem with him, as regards to his bullying me, which was why I moved here. When he got into trouble with the law in Donegal, accusations were made against him. And when those accusations were suspiciously withdrawn, it didn't help my mother and father. Our whole family was ostracised by the local community, which made life very difficult for my mom and dad, who were kind, decent people. The whole family had lived and worked in Donegal for centuries beforehand. That was why I bought the cottage beside the church so they could live out their lives without shame or suspicion."

Mary cringed as he continued saying,

"The accident Brian had in Tenerife was the saddest part, because he had written to my parents. He told them that he was sorting himself out and even had a child that he would introduce to them someday. My mother and father were delighted with the letter, thinking that they had a grandchild; they had always wanted grandchildren. But all that joy was taken away from them when we got the terrible news of his death. They had found several passports in his possession, so even if we tried to find out if indeed, he had a child, we wouldn't have a clue where to start searching. We wouldn't know what country the child might be living in."

What he said next nearly made Mary tell Sean the truth about Rosemary, he said,

"Of all the hurt and lies Brian told over the years, bringing up his parents' hopes, only to then dash them down again. They genuinely felt that this time, he might have been trying to change for the better. But I personally didn't believe it."

After a long silence between the two of them, Sean lifted his head and, smiling at Mary, he said,

"Sorry for the sad story, but enough about Brian and his lies. What about you, are you enjoying life??

Mary was glad to change the subject; she told him about living in Stonybatter, and how she loved living there beside the big smoke. Sean said that from time to time, he had to attend conferences in Croke Park GAA headquarters. He then asked Mary if, if he were up in Dublin, would she meet him for a coffee, and maybe show him a few of the sites. Then their eyes met, and Mary smiled at Sean, answering,

"Gladly."

29

As Mary drove home from the funeral, happily, her thoughts drifted back to Sean and how he had shown her around Ardmore before she left. After breakfast, he came to meet her to say goodbye. But before she left, he suggested a little tour around the town. Mary was in no hurry to head back and felt comfortable in his company. They strolled past the pier where children were fishing for mackerel. Mary smiled to hear the children squealing with delight when they caught a fish. As they carried out along the cliff walk, the sun shone and the gentle breeze made the ferns wave as they passed by. Sean showed her the old, ruined seminary dating back to the year 431, and the holy well where the story was told. If you sat in the stone seat, it would help you get pregnant. Mary laughed and said she wouldn't sit there so. As they carried on their walk, he pointed out the old Coast Guard station that was derelict. It was a very imposing old house that was built around 1867 and was continually manned until the

Civil War in 1922, when the Republicans burned it down. Mary was enjoying the stroll further out on the peninsula. She loved the colours of the gorse and heathers while watching the majestic cormorant stand on a ledge, expanding its wings. Further out on the Cliff, the weather was calm until they reached the lookout post overlooking the Celtic Sea. Sean explained that it was used during World War two by Coast Watch personnel to log all ships and aircraft that passed. When they turned at that point of the Cliff, suddenly the wind from the Atlantic Ocean caught Mary's breath. She watched and laughed as Sean's bright red hair was blown madly in the wind. Sean laughed, also trying to smooth it down. Mary was mesmerised by an ancient round tower, standing nearly one hundred feet high, built in the twelfth century. It was surrounded by an old graveyard that is still used to this day. Also, the ruins of the cathedral, built in the eleventh century on the site of St Declan's monastery, with its religious stone etchings. They descended back down to the village in time for lunch. Mary marvelled at the thatched cottages and the beauty of the whole walk that took them around in a full circle. While having lunch, Sean told her about Ardmore winning the pride of place trophy and how happy he was to live in such a lovely village. Mary agreed, saying that Stoneybatter, where she lived, had won the pride of place also, even though it was in the middle of a city. Before Mary headed home, Sean insisted, she called in to say goodbye to his parents. They stopped by and were invited in for tea before she left. The newly built cottage facing out to Ardmore Bay was lovely and bright with modern underfloor heating and solar panels on the roof. Mary looked around at the photos on the wall and spotted a photograph of Sean and Brian. They were about seven years old, and she still couldn't tell them apart. When she looked at Sean's mum and dad, she thought to herself that they were about the same age as Rose and Frank, but worlds apart from each other in the way they dressed. Before she left for home, Kate gave her freshly baked brown bread and apple tart straight from the oven. Mary felt they were a warm, loving couple that radiated happiness and love.

After the funeral, and as weeks passed, Mary thought the whole situation with Brian would go away. She believed that she could put the past behind her and move on. But she was sadly mistaken. Although from time to time she would get texts from Sean, and that made her heartbeat faster. She told her mother about seeing Sean-Og in the church and passing out from fright. Rose laughed at Mary's story because she had a dream where Mary was walking with a red-headed man by the seashore. They both laughed out loud at the coincidence, but Mary wondered what the dream might have meant. She then went on to tell Rose about Sean's parents and what he had told her about having to leave Donegal. She said that she had felt very sorry for them both for the circumstances Brian had put them in. As the realisation hit her, Rose suddenly put her hand on Mary's arm, stopping her from talking. Wide-eyed and with her mouth open smilingly, the words caught in her throat as she uttered,

"For fucks sake, Mary, they are Rosemary's grandparents, and Sean is her uncle."

Mary nodded yes, but the gravity of her sentence being spoken out loud like that frightened her a little. She told her mother that she was very perplexed; she didn't know what to do for the best. She continued that she couldn't decide whether to break all ties with Sean's family or let them know who Rosemary was. As they sat together trying to reason out the situation Mary was in, Rose spoke first, saying,

"Take all the time you need on your decision, pet, because there could be a lot of repercussions in what you decide for Rosemary, you, and our family."

30

A few days later, Mary received a text from Sean saying he would be in Dublin for the weekend, staying at the Croak Park hotel. He continued that he would be in conferences during the day, but would be free during the night. He asked her if she was interested in meeting on Saturday night; he would love to see her again. Mary was bewildered; she didn't know how she was going to answer his text. She also felt that cutting off all ties with Sean's family would not be fair to Rosemary. She knew that she was the most important person in her decision. She also felt that Sean, Kate, and Sean-Og were good and decent people who deserved to know the truth. Then she thought to herself, what about Sean? What sort of relationship was he expecting? Mary felt that there was some sort of a spark between them, but did she want to let that spark ignite? She decided to meet him and texted him back that she would meet him under the Spire in O'Connell Street. Sean replied with a thumbs-up emoji.

Having dropped Rosemary off with Rose for a sleepover, Mary stood by the Spire waiting. As she waited, her thoughts drifted back to the first time she met Brian. She remembered the excitement of seeing him drive up to the curb in his big red Mustang. Then, he introduced her to Ed and helped her get her first job on the campus. She also remembered how it all went so horribly wrong when Brian got himself into the drug running. It was then her skin started to go cold, and as panic set in, she wanted to run. She felt she was making another stupid, naive decision and wanted to get away.

As she was just about to bolt down Henry Street, Sean pulled up in front of her, blocking her escape. He was on a Dublin touring bike wearing a cycle helmet. Mary was amused as she saw Sean holding his bike and smiling with his trousers tucked into his socks. It was utterly different to Brian's red mustang, she thought to herself. He is entirely different from Brien, as she smiled back at Sean while he put his helmet into his backpack and released his socks from his trousers. Sean looked up at Mary, and her heart skipped a beat as he smiled and asked her, What did she fancy doing? The night was filled with laughter as they toured around the city. They hopped from bar to bar in Dublin's lively scene, stopping for finger food from sidewalk chip vans.

The whole night was magical, and Mary couldn't remember when she had so much fun. When the night came to an end, Mary stood by a taxi door that Sean was holding open for her. As she was just about to get in, Sean leaned over to kiss her goodnight. Suddenly, Mary froze and pulled back. Sean realising that he might have gotten the wrong vibe and had overstepped the mark, drew back and apologised. Mary tried to counter this by saying that she was sorry, as it was not him, but her. On the drive home, she asked herself repeatedly, Should I have let him kiss me, or did I do the right thing?

As she thought some more about why she froze, she realised that when she saw Sean leaning in for the kiss, she also saw Brian's face. She knew that if she were ever to form a relationship with Sean, or any man, she would have to forget about Brian completely. Sean was the absolute opposite of Brian, even if he was his twin, but the question was? Could she get past that and form a loving relationship without any ghosts? When she got home, Mary's phone beeped. It was Sean. His text said that he had a fantastic night and was sorry if he offended her in any way. He continued that he would be returning home tomorrow by the evening train and wondered if she would like to meet for coffee beforehand. He finished by saying that if she didn't want to meet him again, no offence would be taken. The text ended with a kiss emoji. Mary didn't answer while she thought things through; she needed time to think and to sleep on what she was going to do next.

31

Night-terrors never really left her, and that night, while she slept, they came again. She was sitting in a restaurant at a round table, trembling in fear. Seated at the table were she, Rosemary, Rose, and Frank. Brian was standing over them with that same silly grin on his face. Their hands were on the table in front of them and were shackled together by a gold chain. The locks on the chain were made from golden Panthers. Frantically, Mary tried to break the chain and save her family. But the harder she tried, the tighter the chain became. She looked around in despair for a way out but couldn't find one. Mary wanted to grab her daughter and run, but the shackles were too tight. Then, as the cloud lifted, she could see more clearly. She looked up pleadingly into Brian's face, begging for mercy. As she looked closer into his face, she realised that it wasn't Brian. It was Sean-Og ... he was smiling down on her, giving her confidence. Then she looked to Rose and Frank and realised it was not them. It was Kate and

Sean, his parents. She looked down at the gold chain and watched as it started to melt away. Then, a waitress stood beside her to take her order. When she looked up, she was relieved and happy to see her grandmother smiling down at her. Mary opened her eyes and smiled also.

It was early when Mary texted Sean. Her text read.

"Dear Sean. I am sorry for the way we parted last night, as I have some unresolved issues in my life. But to be able to put them behind me, I would have to meet you privately to discuss them. Only then could I be able to move forward. So, if you would like to meet with me again, please let me know."

She finished the text with another kiss emoji.

Immediately, Sean replied, yes, yes, I would love to see you again. Mary responded to Sean, sending him her home address. Within the hour, a taxi pulled up outside Mary's house, and she had fresh coffee brewing as she let him in. Sean looked apprehensive as he sat down, and Mary joined him, saying that she had a story to tell him. When she was ready, she asked Sean not to interrupt her until she had finished. Sean nodded his agreement as he sat back in his seat expectantly with his hands clasped. Mary began telling him about a young girl starting out in life with aspirations of travel, adventure, and fun. She told him about meeting a lovely, handsome man on the plane and falling madly in love with him. But that man turned out to be a monster who dealt in murder, rape, and drugs. She told how she was groomed, coerced, and held captive in his vicious world. She went on to tell him of her escape while carrying his child, and how he followed her to Tenerife to retrieve his stolen Irish Passport. She explained that she had taken the passport so he could not follow her out of Mexico. When he caught up with her, he wanted to turn her and her daughter into drug pushers as well. Sean listened silently and intently as Mary continued her story. As Mary stopped for a second, she took a deep breath before carrying on. She knew that this part would be the most challenging part to tell. It was then she told him about being in the house when Brian had his fatal accident. She explained that to protect her daughter and herself from this monster, she did nothing to help him. She knew it was their only chance of escaping him forever. She finished by saying that the only reason she was telling him all this was because she had met him and his lovely family. She told him that his family were the complete opposite of the beast she had met nearly five years earlier. She continued saying, by telling you all this now, knowing you have a niece and your parents have a grandchild, living in this county, will help you to stop your search. She lives with me here, in this house, and her name is Rosemary. At this stage of my life, my daughter and I are happy. We don't want to jeopardise our happiness with any more ugliness from the past. I also feel, if you never want to contact me again, I will quite understand. But, in making your decision, I would also ask if you would keep all that I have told you private, even between your parents. I know it is a lot to lay on you now, but I also know if there was to be a future between us, you should know everything.

When Mary was finished, there was total silence in the room. Sean sat wide-eyed at what he had just been told. He tried to digest the whole sorry story of what his only brother had put this lovely girl through. Then, as he came to a decision, he apologised to Mary for the way his brother had behaved. Mary thanked him for his apology and for his empathy as he listened to her story. Sean thought of his mother and father and how they both loved and cherished the memory of Brian. He knew he would never be able to reveal to them the awful story he had just been told.

Regarding Rosmary, that would have to wait until another day when he had more time to think. He asked Mary if it was all alright with her, could he have time to consider his answer? He promised her that whatever decision he came to, he would always keep her secret safe. Mary was hoping he would say that and gladly agreed. As Sean left, he stopped and thanked her again for her honesty and strength of character in telling him the whole story. As Mary stood by the open door to let him out, Sean leaned over and kissed her on the cheek. Mary let him, before closing the door.

Two weeks had passed as Mary waited for any word from Sean, but nothing came, not even a text or phone call. She had decided to forget Sean and move on with her life. She was much happier now, having told her story and that terrible weight had been lifted off her shoulders. Also, all the night terrors had diminished. One morning as she came downstairs, she saw an envelope lying on the hall floor. As she picked it up quizzingly, and seeing it was addressed to her, she brought it to the table to read. She opened it to find it was a handwritten letter from Sean. Mary slowly read its content,

Dearest Mary.

I am sorry I have not written earlier. I have been thinking of you and the terrible way my brother had treated you. I was too embarrassed to make contact sooner, feeling that you would want to forget about him and our family forever. I understand how you would like to put the past behind you.

But Mary, from the time I wake in the morning, to the last moment before I fall asleep. You are in my thoughts, and I cannot get you out of my mind. From the first moment we met, I have been captivated by your grace, beauty, and strength. I feel we have a connection that cannot be denied. If by any chance you would consider giving our relationship a go, this would make me very happy. I know that you would not enter this decision lightly, as Rosemary would have to be your number one priority. But your happiness should be considered also, and I would be willing to try everything to make you happy.

This is the only correspondence you will ever receive from me. If you feel that you do not want to keep in contact, I will quite understand. In finishing, I wish you all the love and happiness for the future.

With love.

Sean-Og.

32

It was the following weekend, while Mary was happily brushing Rosemary's beautiful, long auburn hair, she casually asked the question,

"How would you fancy going on a weekend break to the seaside next week? There is somebody I would like to meet"?

Rosemary replied,

"Yippie, I can't wait."

Without telling Kate and Sean how Rosemary was conceived, Mary's heart melted when the introductions were made. She felt that, of all the bad decisions she had made over the years, this decision was one of her best. The tears of joy from everyone, including young Sean, were palpable. Kate and Sean senior dropped to their knees to kiss and hug Rosemary. They now knew for sure that they had met their only grandchild, who they thought was lost forever. They thought they would die without ever knowing her because of the many passports

Brian had in his possession when he had his accident. When they both looked up at Mary with tears in their eyes, they thanked her repeatedly before hugging Rosemary again. Although young Sean had warned them that something extraordinary was about to happen in the form of good news, they never expected how exceptional it was going to be.

Rosemary just took the introductions in her stride. To her, she was just being introduced to her two new grandparents and wondered what all the big fuss was about. But what Rosemary really liked was having Sean as her uncle because he was so full of fun. He would take her out on the rib around Ardmore Cliffs so she could see all the wild birds and sometimes even whale and seal watching. He also taught her how to fish from the harbour and the flat rock. And because he was so popular, she had made loads of new friends in the GAA Club playing camogie and football. She joined the Kayak Club and was also learning how to swim in the boat cove.

It was on such a lovely summer's day when the sun shone and a light breeze caressed the grasses and heathers around them. Mary and Sean sat together on the bank above the flat rock while Rosemary was casting out her fishing line, trying to catch a mackerel. As they rested their heads, looking up at the cloud formations passing, Sean turned to Mary. He reminded her again of how happy she had made his parents. Sean stopped talking for a moment, hesitant about what he was going to say next, before sitting up again while looking down into Mary's eyes. Then he began,

"Mary, I know we have skirted around this question before. I also know that by the answer you gave me, you said that in all or any decisions you made, the most important person in your life would be Rosemary. Someday, Rosemary will grow up and want to make a life of her own. But what about your life here and now, where do you see your future and happiness going forward?" Mary pondered her answer as she looked up at Sean. Before she could answer, Sean continued,

"Look, Mary, I've come to love you and Rosemary more than life itself. I also feel that you have some of the same feelings for me. If you would consider marrying me, I would spend the rest of my life loving you as well as being the happiest man on earth. You don't have to answer immediately, but would you at least consider my proposal?"

Mary closed her eyes for a second to consider, and when she opened them again to answer Sean, he was gone. She sat up to see him standing beside Rosemary, excitedly coaxing her to keep the rod up while she landed her catch. As she watched the two of them shout for joy as Rosemary held up her fish in triumph, she laughed out loud.

33

The Don was pacing, and when the Don paced, people got nervous. As the goons sat around his big, heavy oak table, sweating, some of them trembled. They feared for themselves and their families, knowing that if his anger came down on them, their whole existence could end in an instant. As the Don paced angrily around the seated goons, he waved his hands in the air, agitated, then he pointed at his men, looking for answers or suggestions.

"Nine months ... nine fucking months ... I have been waiting on this shipment. Half a million dollars, and no return."

He cast his eyes suspiciously at his men, but nobody met his eye, and nobody spoke. Everyone sat with their heads bowed, thinking and hoping that the Don's eyes would not rest on them. They were hopeful the scapegoat would be someone else as he passed behind their seats. Suddenly, a shaking voice came from the end of the table, it was like a whisper,

"What about Skip? He was the Irishman's sidekick."

The Don stopped pacing and spun around to look at who had spoken. The goon who spoke continued fearfully and respectfully,

"Skip worked with the Irishman; they were a team together before the barmaid broke them up. He knew how the Irishman worked before his accident. Why not send him to Morocco to complete the deal? He owes us big time. Then afterwards, we can dispose of him, cleaning up the whole mess that Brian created by dying."

Everyone lifted their heads in hopeful agreement while looking at the Don. The Don was thinking, he stopped and looked out the window. He was watching his children running and playing in the compound of his lavish hacienda. His armed guards kept watch over them on the surrounding walls. Nobody spoke as he pondered the suggestion about Skip. He stood scratching his sweaty black beard, thinking until he made his decision. Then, to the goon's relief, he said,

"OK, amigos, get this Skip down here, I want to talk with him."

Skip was delighted when he was informed that the Don wanted to see him. Things were not so good between him and the Don after that bitch Mary broke up their smuggling team. He hated her all the more for having Marisol killed by Brian. Skip and Marisol had a thing together that suited them both whenever they got lonely. But now, since Brian's accident, Skip was like a bottom feeder, scratching out a living selling small deals here and there to losers. On the drive down to Tijuana, Skip was in high spirits, wondering if he was about to get rich again, bringing back consignments of drugs for distribution. When he reached the Don's hacienda, he was strip-searched for any weapons or listening devices he might have hidden on his person. Then, he was told to go into a lavish bathroom and take a shower. Afterwards, he was told to dress in a jumpsuit and slippers left out for him on a table. When he was finally ready, the Don's bodyguards checked him over again before escorting him into the house proper. This was the first time he had ever set foot inside the hacienda. He was very excited, thinking that he must have been selected for a very important role in the organisation. He followed the guard to the meeting room. As he walked, he marvelled at the opulence of his surroundings. He was shown into a room with plush leather settees and armchairs. There were heavy oak furnishings everywhere. The guard told him to sit down and wait, then he left the room.

Moments later, the Don entered the room, and Skip jumped up to a standing position, respectfully. The Don smiled at Skip as he crossed the floor and opened a fancy glass display cabinet full of assorted liquor. He offered Skip a drink while pouring himself a scotch whiskey. Not wanting to offend the Don, Skip said he would have the same. As the Don poured their drinks and plopped two ice cubes into each glass, he told Skip to sit down and make himself comfortable. Skip did as he was told as the Don placed his drink on the table in front of him. When the Don was seated, he eyed Skip suspiciously, but smiling at the same time, which made Skip feel very uncomfortable. They sat together for some time before the Don spoke,

"So, Skip, tell me, what do you know about Morocco?"

Skip was dumbstruck; he didn't know what to say or how to react. He replied,

"I know Brian was sent there to confirm a deal, but he died after an accident before he could complete it. I don't know anything after that, as we had parted company when our smuggling team broke up over Brian losing his Irish passport."

The Don answered,

"Yes, when his passport was stolen, that was very inconvenient for me; I had to procure him new documents to cross over the border. But that was long ago and is now in the past. Brian did rise from the ashes of that bad situation to become a trusted partner in our organisation. Do you think you would be capable of following in his footsteps?"

When Skip heard this, his eyes widened, and he answered enthusiastically,

"Yes, Sir, it would be an honour to work for you and your organisation again. You would find me diligent and hardworking in whatever task you set me."

The Don looked pleased with his answer, while smiling and nodding at Skip, then he said,

"Well, maybe I have a job for you, and if you succeed at this, there could be a bright future ahead for you in our organisation."

Skip was delighted with his answer and knew that whatever the Don wanted him to do, he would perform that task to the best of his ability to regain his trust. Then he thought to himself excitedly,

"Hey everyone ... I'm back in business."

The Don told him that he would travel to Rabat in Morocco. He explained that there was a container in the port waiting to be exported to New York. His job was to make sure all paperwork was completed in Rabat for the loading of the container onto a cargo ship. Once it was in transit, his assignment was complete, and they would take over when it reached New York. Skip was surprised he had to travel to Morocco because he was expecting to be shifting consignments of drugs back across the border to LA. When he mentioned this to the Don, he stood up angrily, saying,

"I thought you said that you would be hardworking and diligent in any task I set you?"

Skip suddenly realised he had said the wrong thing; he had put himself in great danger by questioning the Don. He knew that if he refused to do his bidding, his body would be found in his burned-out car, in some remote part of Mexico. So, he countered,

"No, no, sir, all I meant to say was that I was surprised to be given such an important task to prove my loyalty to you, and I am very appreciative of your offer."

The Don was appeased and sat down again to Skips' relief.

34

Within a few days, and feeling very pleased with himself, Skip sat in a first-class seat sipping champagne while flying to Morocco. He had a big wad of cash at his disposal to pay for any bribes or extra expenses he would encounter. He was to travel as a tourist, staying in a four-star hotel near the port of Rabat. His brief was to go sightseeing around Medina and the tanneries of Marrakesh. Here, he would meet his contact, who would arrange to show him the container for transporting. After all the documentation was completed, he was to stay close and ensure it was loaded onto the container ship. Once the boat had sailed, his job was done, and he was to confirm everything with the Don personally. He had an open-ended ticket for his return to LA at his own leisure.

The job went without a hitch, and Skip, feeling very relaxed and happy with how things had worked out, decided to stay on for another couple of days. His contact, named Nabil, seemed like a nice guy and said he would show him around some of the Souqs and Almoravid Qubba, the oldest monument in Marrakesh. Skip was enjoying his tour as they drove from Rabat to Marrakesh. But suddenly, on a quiet dusty road, the car was pulled over by the driver. Nabil stuck a gun into Skip's ribcage, telling him to get out of the vehicle. Skip knew at that moment that he was never to be allowed to return to America, and his disappearance had already been arranged when the job was completed. Standing by the roadside with his hands up, Skip was thinking hard. When Nabil told him to walk towards the desert, he knew what was coming next, so he started to bargain for his life. He told Nabil that he had no intention of returning to America, as he had set up his own drug operation in Europe. He continued tempting Nabil by saying,

"I could make you a wealthy man supplying me with goods for my new market, and the Don need never know about our partnership."

Nabil stood thinking with the gun pointed at Skip, as he stood in the oppressive heat of the sun, with sweat trickling down his back. Nabil eventually asked,

"OK, what did you have in mind?"

And Skip knew that he would live another day.

He spun a story about transporting millions of dollars in hash to Europe through the many contacts Nabil had in Marrakesh. As Nabil listened, wide-eyed and greedy, Skip slowly approached him with his hands still in the air, explaining how rich he was going to make him. When he got close enough, he grabbed the gun while punching Nabil in the face. Having disarmed him, he told the driver to get out of the car, and the two men stood at the side of the road begging for mercy. Skip did consider killing both men, but as he thought, he knew that if he returned to LA, he would surely be killed by the Don's men. He knew that his only option was to keep on running and make a new life for himself, but where? He remembered that Brian travelled from Morocco to Tenerife, but why? Was he setting up some business for himself that ended when he had his accident? If so, what was the business, and who was his contact? With minimal persuasion and thinking he was going to be a rich man, Nabil was able to supply him with a shipment of drugs and the name of a local contact in Tenerife. When he got there, Skip thought that his contact would have been the same person that Brian had been dealing with. But he was disappointed when he was told that nobody had ever heard of any other contact. Skip wasn't deterred; he felt that if Brian were involved in a caper, it would be more lucrative than his. As Skip made more contacts in Tenerife, he inquired about Brian, but every road led to a dead end. His frustration was getting the better of him as he felt he was missing something, but the answer kept eluding him. Months had passed, until one night, Skip stopped by the Queen Vick for a meal and to see a drag show that was recommended to him. At this stage, he had given up his search of ever finding out who Brian's contact was. Anyway, now, he was doing ok with his own supplier. He was mainly dealing with tourists around the shady areas, passing quick deals, but he still dreamt of the big times. The Queen Vick wasn't his type of venue, but he had seen most of the other acts in the area and felt he had nothing to lose by going. The show was entertaining, and the food was tasty. There was also a good buzz in the bar. During the interval, he decided to use the toilet. As he passed through the lobby to get to the gents, there were framed photos of different drag queens, staff members, and customers displayed on the wall. He stopped in disbelieve at one in particular, there in the photo, smiling back at him, was Brian and Mary, they were standing behind the bar smiling. He had to take a second look as he couldn't believe his eyes. Taking out his phone, he took a few photos of the photograph before returning to his seat. When he sat down again, he opened his phone to zoom in on Brian's face before saving the image. When the waitress came with his bill at the end of the night, Skip, giving her a big tip, showed her the photo and said that the guy was a friend of his. The waitress, happy with her tip, said,

"That is Sean and Mary, they live in Ireland, but they come here regularly to help out behind the bar with their daughter Rosemary."

When Skip left the bar, he was furious, and as he walked and thought, his hatred for Mary became stronger. That fucking bitch broke up our successful business back in the States. Then she fucked-up our relationship with the Don, leaving me high and dry. It is because of her; I am here on this god-forsaken island, scratching out a meagre existence. Then, my long-time partner plans his own death to escape the cartel to hook up with her again. As Skip concluded while smiling to himself, So that's it, I have solved the puzzle. Mary did a runner from Mexico to set up the business. Then, when the time was right, Brian followed her from Morocco to arrange his so-called accident here. When everything was settled, they moved back to Ireland to continue their new business together. Very ingenious, but what is the caper? Who is the contact? How much money is to be made? And where do I fit in?

35

Mary was twisting and turning as she slept; she was moaning and calling out incoherently. In her dream, the night was cloudy and dark as the driving rain lashed against her face and eyes, blurring her vision. As she looked down, she could see her knuckles were cold and white from gripping the side of the small boat as it rocked violently from side to side in the raging black sea, as the wind howled. Suddenly, she was thrown from the boat into the cold water. While splashing about, choking, and gasping for air, she knew she was drowning, and a hand appeared in front of her face. Reaching up to grab it, she looked up to see her grandmother saving her. She felt her strength and assurance return as she looked into her grandmother's eyes, reassuring her to take heart. Then her eyes opened to see Sean lying beside her in the bed, holding her hand, calming her racing heart. He smiled at her lovingly, saying that she was having a bad dream and everything was alright now. Relieved that he was there with her, she placed her head onto his chest. Mary relaxed, but was concerned because it had been a long time since she had had a bad dream like that, as she pondered what it meant. Sunday mornings were a quiet time on Oxmanstown Road, as Mary and Sean sat at the table drinking tea and reading the morning papers. Rosemary was on a sleepover with Frank and Rose whenever Sean stayed. But the weekend was coming to an end as Sean was on duty from Monday at the coastguard station and had to get the evening train back.

Mary would be sad to see him go; she felt that they were very easy together. If Sean weren't staying with her, she would be staying with him in his small cottage he had rented. Or they would be holidaying in Tenerife during the mid-term breaks with all the family. Rosemary loved visiting her nana Kate and her grandad Sean in Ardmore. She had so much freedom there and had made many friends in the GAA club. Sean would teach her how to swim in the open sea off the boat cove wall. He also taught her how to fish from the rib, or the flat rock, and she would always want to carry home her own catch proudly.

Mary also took up sea-swimming; she loved the invigoration and motion of the waves as she swam. She enjoyed jogging around the cliff top as well, to keep her fitness level in tip-top condition. At one stage, Sean did suggest again that maybe they might consider moving in together, or even marriage. But life at the moment prohibited that because Mary wanted to take things slow. Rosemary was happily settled at school in Stoneybatter. Mary was moving into her final year at the Law Library in preparation for her calling to the bar. If he wanted, Sean would be able to get a transfer to Dublin as a fire officer. But it would mean leaving his mum and dad alone, as well as leaving his coaching position, and being a coast guard, which he loved most of all. So, they both agreed, for the moment, they would continue as they were because they were so happy together. In the meantime, in the mid-Atlantic Island of Tenerife, Skip was covertly gathering information about the couple. He started a relationship with one of the waitresses and frequented Queen Vick. By now, he knew who owned the business, who ran it, and the dates Brian and Mary would visit Tenerife. But, more importantly, he acquired Mary's address in Dublin. He still couldn't figure out what their operation was, who their supplier was, or the contact. To him, everything looked kosher, but he felt that he was somehow missing that final piece in the puzzle. Then he thought, maybe the contact is situated in Ireland, perhaps I am looking in the wrong place. Knowing Brian, he is probably supplying the whole of Europe through the back door of Ireland while making a killing. Maybe I should visit them there and continue our partnership.

36

It was a lovely sunny morning; Mary had met Rose in the Phoenix Park, and they went jogging together. They did this by arrangement, then they would stop for a coffee, have a chat, and afterwards, jog home to their respective homes. While in the coffee shop, Rose told Mary that she was not sleeping well and felt something was wrong. Mary felt the same but didn't tell her that the night-terrors had returned. Rose continued inquiring if everything was good between Sean and her. Mary just smiled and shrugged her shoulders, saying that they were fine. She even told Rose about Sean's proposal and their decision to wait. Rose seemed appeased but still looked perturbed. As Rose rubbed the back of her neck, still feeling something was wrong, she inquired about Mary's exams. But Mary again replied that all was going fine and to stop worrying about nothing. Mary asked her mother if she might be worried about Frank? But Rose just waved her suggestion away, saying that he was fine, too, so they let the conversation drop. Later, when they finished their coffee, they kissed each other goodbye, agreeing that they would meet again during the week. As Mary slowly jogged home, she pondered their conversation. She knew life was good now, but still had a feeling of dread in her stomach, and her mother, feeling the same as her, didn't help. Suddenly, a man appeared jogging beside her and said,

"Hello Mary, isn't it a lovely sunny day to be out exercising?"

When she turned and saw Skip running beside her, she almost buckled. Keeping the pace, he smiled at her and said,

"How is Brian, or should I say, Sean?"

He continued threateningly,

"I wonder if the Don would like to know that his favourite right-hand man didn't die in Tenerife after all. And I'm sure he would be interested in his whereabouts, and the company he was keeping."

Mary was dumbfounded; she had stopped running to face him, and all she could answer was,

"Brian is dead, I promise."

But she knew by the look on Skip's face that he didn't believe her. Skip knew that by mentioning the Don, he would get her attention. He also knew that if the Don ever found out that he (Skip) was alive, it would mean certain death for him. But he wasn't about to tell Mary that, so he answered,

"Yeah, yeah, I know you two have some sweet deal going on here. I also know that you owe me big time for cutting me out before. But I'm back now and ready to do business, so I think we should form up our little team as before. And just to let you both know, I am not here by accident; the Don knew that there was something shady about Brian's so-called accidental death."

Skip took out his phone to show Mary. He showed her the photos of her, Sean, and Rosemary in Tenerife. Then, when he saw the look of fear on her face, he continued,

"Look, I'm not greedy or avaricious, all I'm looking for is my fair share of the business as before, as well as the names of your contact and supplier. But if you try and cut me out again or cross me, there will be severe consequences for you and Brian. I am also aware that Brian has some contacts with the Coast Guard who help him land the shipments. As you can see, I'm well up to speed on all your dealings, so don't think for one minute you can fool me."

Then he finished by saying,

"I'll be staying in Dublin for the next while, keeping a sharp eye on you. If I were you, I wouldn't do, or say, anything stupid, until we talk again."

Then he just turned and jogged away, leaving Mary standing and shaking alone in the park. Mary didn't know what to do, whether to run after her mother or go home and lock herself away in the house. While she was thinking and hoping that she was having a nightmare again, she hoped it would all go away when she woke up beside Sean. Her thoughts turned to Rosemary and her safety, as she could feel the panic rising in her body. She tried to calm herself and think logically. As she walked home slowly, she was trying to rationalise this awful situation she found herself in. She figured that Skip didn't know where Sean lived; otherwise, he would have contacted him first. But the fact that he knew Sean worked as a coast guard put him and his job in jeopardy. She also feared that if the Don found out Brian, and not Sean, was still alive, he would surely have him assassinated. Mary knew that by being an innocent man, and his brother's identical twin, Sean was in very great danger without even knowing it. Mary decided, for everyone's sake, she would say nothing until Skip contacted her again. She knew Skip was greedy and wanted in on what he thought was a lucrative drug business. So, he wouldn't have informed the Don yet about Brian being alive, at least until he got his big payout, which meant she had time to think.

37

Over the next few weeks, Mary went back to constantly checking behind herself. Every window, mirror, or anything reflective, she checked, but nothing showed up. She thought she would go mad waiting for Skip to make contact again. She would also put off Sean visiting her in Dublin, giving the excuse that Rosemary was taking part in a school play. Or Rosemary was missing Kate and Sean senior, and she was coming down to visit them instead. But before she would set off for Ardmore, she would double-check that nobody was following her. Rose also picked up that Mary was acting strangely, with agitated moods and was harassing her to find out if something was wrong. Mary, trying not to explode, would smile and say that she had upcoming college exams and was a little stressed. It was six weeks before Skip made contact again, and Mary was glad because she could not take the waiting anymore. He told her that he had set up a deal that would make them all rich. He also said that if everything went according to plan, she and Brian would never see or hear from him again.

But again, he threatened her by saying,

"If the plan went wrong, for any reason, I would contact the Don. I would have no hesitation in telling him about Brian, you, and your daughter Rosemary."

Mary nodded her agreement, knowing that the time had come to tell Sean about the danger they were all in. As they sat at her table in Stoneybatter, Sean was ashen-faced to hear the story as he looked at her in disbelieve. After a long time thinking in silence, he lifted his head, saying,

"We will both have to meet this man and find out what he wants to make him go away."

Mary wasn't sure that Sean was making the right move, she countered,

"If you meet Skip now, he will know for sure that you were not Brian. He might pull out of the deal altogether and inform the Don in retaliation. The Don would see you in the photo and see Brian; he wouldn't care it was you. He would have you killed, and maybe me, and Rosemary also."

Mary continued sadly, while taking Sean's hand in hers,

"Oh, Sean, I am so sorry for bringing all this evil into your life. If I had known what was to happen, I would never have gotten involved with you or your lovely family."

Sean's eyes softened as he gripped Mary's hand, gently saying,

Mary, my love, my everything, you and Rosemary are my family now. I wouldn't have it any other way. Somehow, we will rise above this terrible thing that has come to visit us united as a family. But most importantly, I want you to know that it was never you who brought evil to our door. It was all my brother Brian's doing. The only thing you brought into my life was love and happiness. I will always be grateful to you for that, no matter what happens in the future."

By the end of the conversation, they both had agreed that, no matter what situation was presented to them, they would face it as one loving unit. It was a further two weeks before the meeting took place. Skip sat across from Sean, totally astonished and bemused. He couldn't believe his eyes, thinking that two brothers could look so much alike, but he didn't care. All Skip wanted was to get his plan agreed on; he didn't care if he was dealing with Jack-the-lad, once he got what he wanted. He also knew, as he wasn't dealing with Brian, there would be no sharing out of the spoils. He knew that he had this frightened couple in the palm of his hand. He felt the power over them both was enough to seal this deal, and he would be in clover for the rest of his life.

38

When Skip laid out his plan in front of them, Mary gasped in horror, looking at Sean. Sean, with his eyes staring at her, told her not to say a word. They both could see the danger he was going to be put in, not only with his job, but his life. Having read and listened to Skips' plan, Sean nodded his agreement. Mary couldn't believe he was agreeing, but kept quiet as Skip and Sean discussed its viability. Mary then realised that for the past six weeks, Skip hadn't been watching her at all. He had been in Morocco setting up a drugs deal, and she needn't have watched her back at all. It was Sean who interrupted her thoughts by saying,

"So, that's the plan, a shipment of drugs will arrive off the South Coast of Ireland. My job, as a coastguard, is to arrange a small boat to rendezvous undetected with the mother ship. When the shipment is off-loaded, I am to guide it into a pick-up point along the coast for distribution?"

Then Sean turned to Skip and asked earnestly,

"If I perform this task, and everything goes according to plan. Will you forget you ever knew us, and leave us alone to get on with our lives forever?"

Skip answered with conviction,

"Absolutely, you will never see or hear from me again, I promise."

But, in the back of his mind, Skip knew if his plan succeeded, there was no way he would let this fish off the hook. He knew he could make millions in the future by threatening them with the Don. He also made one more critical stipulation before the meeting ended, as he said sneeringly,

"Mary was to accompany them in the boat on the night of the drop. I want to make sure that you stick to your end of the bargain. It would be a pity to have to act if you tried to double-cross me; someone might get hurt or even killed."

Without hesitation, Sean agreed to his terms. The meeting ended with Skip saying that he would be in touch when the transfer of goods was about to take place. Over the next few days, as they waited for Skip to contact them, Sean and Mary walked the cliffs around Ardmore. As they stood on the cliff top with the shelter of the ridge behind their back, Sean pointed out to the flat rock. They had fished there during the summer months, having so much fun with Rosemary. They hugged and kissed before moving on arm and arm, slowly walking around the Round Tower. They reminisced about the first time Mary visited Ardmore as they strolled down into the village. While drinking coffee together, Sean's phone rang, and they both jumped, knowing it was Skip. Mary listened as they spoke. Sean agreed with whatever Skip proposed. But suddenly, Sean cut across Skip, disagreeing with him as he took over the conversation. He told Skip that it was the wrong night and to contact the mother ship. As Skip listened, Sean explained and suggested another night when the weather would be stormy with dark clouds. He also told Skip that he would be off duty that night, and nobody would miss him from the station. Skip agreed with his suggestion, as the night was decided for the drop and the call ended. At around midnight on the night of the drop, Skip arrived at the boat cove driving a stolen van. Sean and Mary were waiting beside a small wooden motorboat with an outboard engine. He had already cut away the chain securing it to the side wall. The night was dark, and the waves lashed the rocks along the cliff face. The squally wind was high, blowing in showers of driving rain. Mary was glad Sean insisted she wear a dry suit to keep her warm against the chill. As the three of them pulled the little boat into the water, Sean whispered to her,

"Remember what I told you about the flat rock, wait for the swell, and then the rise."

Skip noticed them whispering, and he stopped pushing the boat, taking a gun out for them to see. He warned them not to do anything stupid now, or they would both be very sorry. Sean calmed him by saying,

"There is nothing to worry about. I was only warning her to mind her hands as the boat's oars could hurt her."

When they had the boat launched, they rowed out a little past the harbour wall so as not to attract attention, then Sean started the engine. As they made their way along the side of the cliff using the shelter from the wind, Skip seemed to relax a little. At the tip of the cliff, they waited for a signal from the mother ship. Mary's heart was racing, waiting and hoping that this nightmare would end soon.

Then they saw it in the distance, a red light blinking, Sean revved the motorboat out into the Celtic Sea to meet it. The waves lashed and bounced them around as they made their way across to the ship. They pulled along the port side for shelter from the wind. Within minutes, out of the dark, six bales were loaded over the side of the ship into their little boat. Mary watched as the bales settled into the bottom of the boat. She could see the boat getting lower in the water from the extra weight and wondered if the waves would overtop them when they pulled away from the safety of the ship. Then it was time to pull away, as they did so, the full force of the wind and sea hit them. Luckily, it was at their back and pushing them toward the black headland ahead. On the way back, nobody spoke. Mary looked up to see Sean's firm hand on the rudder and took heart.

Skip was at the bow of the boat watching as the headland got nearer. Just then, and out of the blue, a squall hit them from the side. Sean fought hard to steady the boat as the waves threatened to overturn their little boat. The cold rain lashed into Mary's face, blurring her vision. When she looked down at her white hands holding the wet rail of the boat, she had a flashback to her night-terrors. She remembered seeing that same scene again, then being thrown out of the boat. She knew her grandmother wouldn't be there to save her now. She tried breathing hard to keep herself from panicking. Then, as the boat came nearer to the headland, the wind subsided a little, and she took heart again. As she looked up, she could see that they were not heading back towards the harbour, but straight for the cliffs. The white horses were lashing against the rocks in a terrible roar, and the noise was deafening. Skip could see them also; he called out to Sean that they were getting too close to the cliffs. But Sean ignored him and kept the little boat on its course. Skip was getting nervous; he drew his gun in warning to turn the boat around. As he pointed the gun at Sean, he started to rock the boat from side to side, knocking Skip off balance, and he nearly knocked the three of them into the water. Skip roared at Sean over the noise, asking him if he had gone mad, while pointing the gun again. But before he could pull the trigger, Sean rocked the boat again. This time it was so violent that the boat was overturned, and they were all thrown into the raging sea. Mary was gasping for air as she came up. She could see Sean holding onto the side of the capsized boat, and he grabbed her hand. Skip was holding onto the other side of the boat, trying to keep his head above water. Sean called to Mary to follow him as they both swam towards the cliff edge, leaving Skip holding on to the boat. While they swam, he stopped from time to time to make sure she was ok. When they got to the point where he wanted to be, Sean stopped swimming and treaded water. He shouted at Mary to wait for the swell. Suddenly, when it came, they were both lifted as Sean shouted to Mary,

"Swim, now, swim hard for your life."

As they swam, the wave smashed against the flat rock, then receded out again. They were left like two fish out of water, lying on the rock, gasping for air. Before the next wave came crashing in again, Sean grabbed Mary by the arm and shouted at her to get up quickly, then they both scrambled up the bank to safety. While they caught their breath after the waves, Sean took from his pocket a fairy light pistol and fired it up into the sky. He grabbed Mary again by the arm, telling her to keep climbing as fast as she could. When they reached the top of the cliff, Mary and Sean were gasping for air. But Sean wouldn't let her rest; he took her by the hand and pulled her along, running for the roadway that met the cliff walk. From there, he pulled out two bicycles hidden in the ditch. Then, they both freewheeled down past the Round Tower to their cottage in the village. They hid the bikes around the side of the cottage and went inside. As soon as the door was closed, and without turning on the lights, Sean stripped down to his pyjamas and dried his hair. Within minutes, a flashing blue light appeared, and there was a banging on the front door. Sean waited a second before sheepishly opening the door. He was told that there was a distress flare spotted in the bay, and they were launching the lifeboat. Sean answered the caller, saying to give him a minute while he got dressed. As he did so, Mary asked him if he thought that Skip would have survived the capsizing. Before he left, he kissed her on the lips and looked lovingly into her eyes before saying,

"They all had the same chance of living or dying in the water, and Skip knew the danger as they did."

Then he turned and was gone, leaving Mary alone in the house, worrying.

39

Mary couldn't settle; all night long, she paced up and down. When first light came, she felt that she had to go down to the harbour to see what was happening. Her forehead and hands were scraped from being thrown onto the flat rock. The bridge of her nose was also cut and swollen. She knew if she appeared looking like this, concerned neighbours would ask questions as to what had happened to her. She tried to think, and she came up with the idea of leaving the house in the sorry state she was in. She took her bicycle from the side of the cottage and walked beside it to the harbour. When she got there, she could see that a full-scale rescue operation was in progress. A rescue helicopter was hovering overhead, and the RNLI lifeboat was trawling across the bay. There was no sign of Sean's rib; she presumed that they were searching along the cliff face. Garda cars had cordoned off the boat cove with tape around the stolen van. Because it was low tide now, custom vehicles were on the strand gathering in the bales of drugs. As she stood mesmerised at all the commotion around her, Kate appeared beside her. When she saw the state of Mary's face and hands, she was very concerned, asking what had happened to her.

Embarrassed, Mary answered,

"Oh, it's nothing really; I feel like such a fool. I was worried about Sean being out on the RIB in the rough sea all night. When first light came, I had to come down to see that he was ok. But, on the way, the front wheel of my bicycle hit the path. I went over the handlebars and put my hands out to save myself."

Kate, feeling sorry for Mary, tut-tutted her, saying,

"Of course, it was a natural reaction to be worried about Sean, as I was, but the storm has abated now, and they know the shoreline well."

She turned to Mary, saying,

"Come over to the house now, and we'll get you cleaned up, as you will have to look your best when he comes in.

Mary agreed thankfully; the two ladies made their way through the watching crowd, wheeling her bike. In the house, Sean Senior had his ear to the local radio, listening to all the goings-on. Gleefully, he lifted his head from time to time to announce another scrap of important information he had just heard.

Then he lifted his head to announce,

"They had just located poor Johnny Farrissey's fishing boat; it was all broken up in one of the coves."

He continued shaking his head sadly.

"And it's his only source of income; what an awful shame."

The two ladies agreed as they sat by the kitchen table. Mary's heart was racing; she tried to calm herself, but all she wanted to do was run outside again.

Just then, Sean Senior announced again excitedly,

"They have found a body floating in the water."

He continued, "The coast guard is asking for volunteers to walk out along the cliff edge to see if there are any more bodies or survivors."

Mary was only too glad for the excuse to go outside. She told them that she would rather be out doing something to help Sean than drinking tea in the kitchen. Mary knew that the body found was that of Skip, and the broken boat was the one they had used.

The Garda in charge explained that the twelve volunteers would walk the cliffs looking down for anything unusual, either on the rocks or in the water. If they spotted something, they were to stop and put their hand up, then someone would come to investigate. As Mary walked along the cliff-top, she stopped to look across Ardmore Bay. In the distance, she could see the headland of Ring and Helvic Head, the Gaeltacht area of County Waterford. Every time she looked, its beauty always amazed her. She wondered to herself, why would evil men, like Brian and Skip, bring such misery and hardship to hundreds of people in a place of such beautiful scenery? She felt that at this place, she could stop running away because there were no passports and no fear, just love. She felt that her journey had led her here, to this safe spot, where Sean was searching below. As she looked down again, out over the edge of the cliff, she could see Sean's rib searching along the coves, driving in, then reversing out again. She thought of this lovely, gentle man, who, without a moment's hesitation, would give his life to save others. She also knew that if Skip hadn't been found dead, Sean would have given his own life to save him. And it would have been the same for any of his companions in the RNLI; she felt pride for those wonderful men and women in the job they did. At that moment, her heart was bursting with love for Sean. She wanted to call down to him at the top of her voice to let him know she was there. But she knew it would be futile because of the height she was up and the screeching seagulls soaring below her. By late afternoon, and as nothing else was found, they started to wind down the rescue operation. Mary was totally exhausted, but she wouldn't leave the harbour wall until Sean's rib came in. She knew that he would also be exhausted, having been out all night and day searching up and down the cliff face. When he eventually did come in and the rib was secured for the night, Mary ran to hug and kiss him before he left the pier. To the whistles and jeers of his mates, they walked arm in arm back to their cottage. They slept for nearly twelve hours and would have slept more if a heavy banging on the front door hadn't woken them. As Sean got up to open it, he was greeted by an angry-looking Kate who brushed past him as she walked straight through to the kitchen. As Sean followed her, a concerned Mary joined them while tying her dressing gown. They were both worried that they had missed something about the drop, and it had been found out. As soon as Kate sat down, she angrily asked,

"What were you two thinking of, treating your family in such a manner?"

Mary looked at Sean, afraid to answer. She was thinking that somehow, they had messed up.

Kate interrupted her thoughts, continuing,

"Do you realise that your whole family are at their wits' end with worry trying to contact you? They have been watching the news and the whole drug investigation unfolding. They wanted to know if you and Sean were in any danger and if you were safe."

It was then that Mary realised that before the drop, they both turned off their mobile phones. They left them in the cottage in case something went wrong, and the signal would prove that they never left. A very relieved Mary said,

"I'm so sorry, Kate. My only concern was for Sean when we were woken by the emergency services to mobilise everyone for a rescue operation."

She told Kate that she would immediately turn her phone on and contact her family. When she switched on her phone, she was surprised to see so many missed calls. They came from Tenerife and, of course, her mother, who left a million messages to call her back immediately. Rose answered on the first ring; she was also angry but relieved to speak to her daughter at last. She told Mary how she had been having awful dreams about her and Sean drowning in the Black Sea. She continued that she was afraid to close her eyes in case the night terrors came back. When she had got through to Kate, she told her that they were both ok but exhausted after the search. Rose told Mary that she was very proud of her for volunteering on the cliff searching for bodies. But until she could hear her own daughter's voice, she couldn't rest. Mary apologised to Rose and calmed her as best she could, knowing she was still agitated. She told her mother that the night terrors would definitely go away now, after what had happened in Ardmore and everything turned out for the best. Softly, Mary said that everything was fine now and could even be perfect, as she and Sean were safe and well. A more relaxed Rose smiled while saying to Mary,

"You seem to have found a good man there, Mary. Maybe you should consider him a keeper?"

With Sean and Kate listening to Mary's conversation with Rose, she turned up the speaker so they could hear better. Mary looked into Sean's eyes, answering,

"Mom, he is definitely a very good man, and of course, I feel he is a keeper. And if he were to ask me again to marry him ... I would say yes ... in a heartbeat."

THE END.

Red Of
Rooske Road
Dunboyne
DUNBOYNE ATHLETIC CLUB
CHRISTY KELLY MEMORIAL
ATHLETIC TRACK
Naomh Peadar Dun Boinne
ST. PETER'S DUNBOYNE G.A.A.
Reilig Ruscaigh
ROOSKE CEMETARY
Leabharlann Phoibli
PUBLIC LIBRARY
James Dunne

The year was 1918, and a pandemic called the Spanish flu had spread worldwide causing millions of deaths. A little over one hundred years later another pandemic called Covid 19 has struck again causing the same loss of life and devastation across the world. In Martin's story, he tells of his great Aunt Lily who in 1918 survived the flu in Dunboyne, Co Meath, Ireland. Young and in love with a local lad who her autocratic father believed was beneath her station, she had dreamt of marriage and a home of her own, dreams that slowly crumbled by the heartache of a love taken from her. It was a time when a young lady's single status governed her behaviour and was generally expected to accept her lot in life. After the death of her mother as a result of the flu, a strong-willed Lily decides to take her destiny into her own hands and sets sail on an adventure to find her lost love.

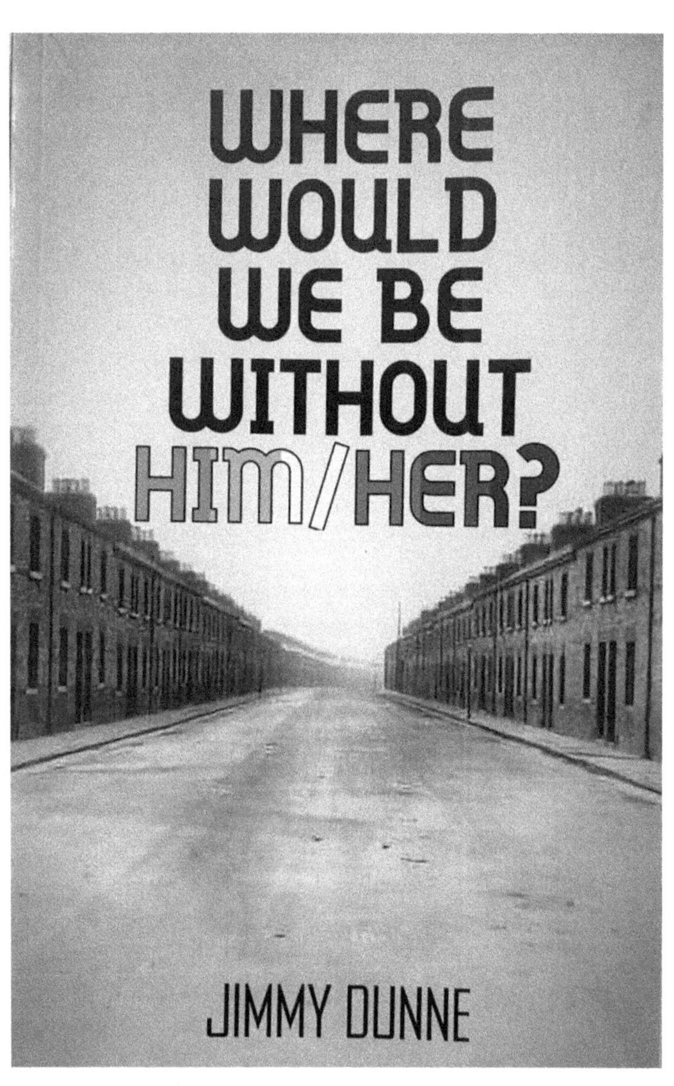

WHERE
WOULD
WE BE
WITHOUT
HIM/HER?
JIMMY DUNNE

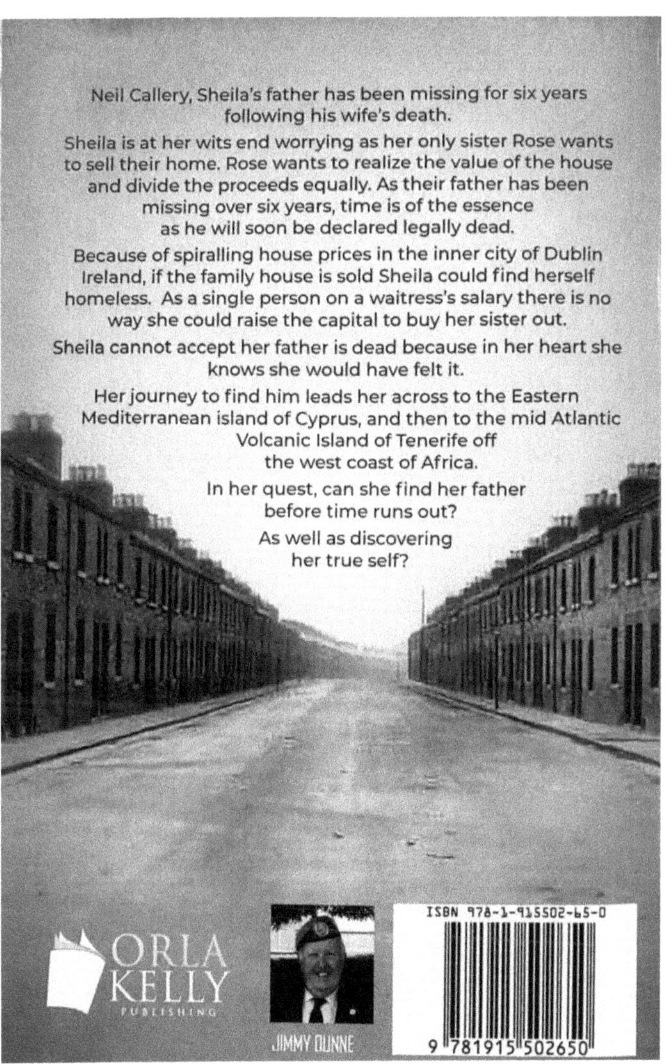

Neil Callery, Sheila's father has been missing for six years following his wife's death.

Sheila is at her wits end worrying as her only sister Rose wants to sell their home. Rose wants to realize the value of the house and divide the proceeds equally. As their father has been missing over six years, time is of the essence as he will soon be declared legally dead.

Because of spiralling house prices in the inner city of Dublin Ireland, if the family house is sold Sheila could find herself homeless. As a single person on a waitress's salary there is no way she could raise the capital to buy her sister out.

Sheila cannot accept her father is dead because in her heart she knows she would have felt it.

Her journey to find him leads her across to the Eastern Mediterranean island of Cyprus, and then to the mid Atlantic Volcanic Island of Tenerife off the west coast of Africa.

In her quest, can she find her father before time runs out?

As well as discovering her true self?

www.ingramcontent.com/pod-product-compliance
Lightning Source LLC
Chambersburg PA
CBHW050441200726
48295CB00024B/780